Manhattan Hitwoman

©2022. EDICO
Edition: JDH Éditions
77600 Bussy-Saint-Georges. France

Printed by BoD - Books on Demand, Norderstedt, Germany

ISBN: 978-2-38127-253-5
Legal deposit: April 2022

Translation from French: Morgane Gey
Cover: Cynthia Skorupa

Pierre Vaude

Manhattan Hitwoman

JDH Éditions

1

I had opened my mailbox with a smile, only retrieving a blank envelope with no address – probably an ad. Taking out a postcard-sized Bristol board, a weird feeling had started to creep up on me.

Leaning on my elbows at the kitchen table, I stir my cup of coffee as I read for the umpteenth time the words written in blue marker on the cheap cardboard. It's hard not to read the seven words over and over again, signed with a pasty hieroglyphic signature. "You white pig, I'll kill you." Simple, straight to the point, but terribly effective for the hack-writer, cookie-cutter prose manufacturer that I am. I turn the card over on the table, refusing to look at the sick handwriting anymore, and gulp down my coffee before putting the empty cup on top as I fight against the itch to tear it up and throw it in the trash. I'm a strong person, but this death threat makes me utterly uncomfortable. No one can ever get used to being a moving target, at least that's what my former years as a reporter have taught me. Clenching my spoon between loose fingers, the autumn sun catches the edge of the window as if nothing had happened.

How could this bitch have found me?

I'm livid, cursing because I don't get it, because it's beyond comprehension. How could she have traced me? She doesn't know about me and I have only spoken of her to two reliable people: my psychiatrist and my friend Archie. It's impossible that either of them would have betrayed me, and if they'd let anything slip about the terrible accident that links me against my will to this spawn, how would she have known about it? It has to be through another source. But which one? And if she knows what happened, how does she not know that I had nothing to do with it? Well, next to nothing.

Thoughts are racing inside my head. This death threat wasn't random. Is she the one who wrote it or am I making up the narrative?

All of a sudden, I'm afraid to go out. Are the streets safe? I've gone through enough dangerous times during my reporter days to know how to deal with stress, but I need to stay alert. I know this girl from my shrink, and I've heard enough to know that she is a real psychopath who can come after me when I least expect it. Getting up to pour myself a drink, I keep thinking that I shouldn't be intimidated and that if I don't go out now, I might stay cooped up forever. I come to my senses: this nutjob is in a cell with bars as big as my wrists, in the psychiatric section of a nearby Manhattan hospital and, given her criminal record, she's not about to get out.

Deciding to venture downtown, I hope that strolling will do me some good and that I'll find a somewhat peace of mind. On Madison, as usual, pedestrians are hurrying, not a single one aware of another's worries. The anonymity that the herd offers is terrifying. The crowd is high on indifference; people follow, cross and avoid their neighbor at the last moment without a glance. Although it should be incredibly distressing, the latent atavism is actually reassuring: we are more serene buried in the pack where our genes can breathe. I avoid their gazes as they do with mine, but my guard is up. I imagine the madwoman disguised as a grim reaper, ready to pounce in the obscurity of a gate, waiting for my oblivious proximity, or her accomplices following me from a few feet behind, a butcher knife between their clenched teeth. Refusing to believe any of it, I let the stream of people carry me. Too much sun, too many pretty women in a haste, wrapped up to fend off the cold, too many loden cloaks, leather jackets, designer wraps and duffel-coats in the parade. Strangely enough, the more passers-by suffocate me, the less stressed and worried I am, even if I still look over my shoulder obsessively. Stopping regularly in front of window shops to check in the reflection if I'm being followed, I quickly learn how to play the chased but I'm anxious, my fists are tight clenched in my pockets, set to strike, and my teeth are gritted, ready to bite.

The sun went into hiding and the autumn air is crisp so I raise the collar of my jacket until the velvet on the leather protects my neck, and the sensation is reassuring. Against my better judgement, I halt my roaming in front of the gun store on Madison, look at the revolvers for a good fifteen minutes, but resist the urge to go in and buy one. I won't be daunted, however, and I feel ready to fight, on the verge of authorizing myself to slay this murderer, this parricide perpetrator (the news channels had turned it into their headlines during her first incarceration). Is the pacifist in me slowly dying? I understand that I'm not more civilized than my neighbors but that my life is much more important than theirs. Who would believe that, just yesterday, I was combatting the NRA[1], fist in the air and fight words pouring from my lips, and that I'm now here, window-shopping before of one of the armories accountable for the recurring shootings?

Hesitating at first, I quickly get my act together. This woman and her death threat are hurting me as it is and that's probably what she wants – to scare me. But she won't have my head nor my body, and I wasn't about to make her job easier. I resume to walk, thinking of going home: I'm uncomfortable and, despite critical thinking, beside reasoning, she's chipping away at my spirit.

Morales…

---

[1] NRA: The National Rifle Association (NRA) is an American 501c41 non-profit civil rights organization dedicated to promoting firearms in the United States and advocating for a non-restrictive interpretation of the Second Amendment to the U.S. Constitution.

Unaware of my own doings, I whisper her name in a low voice. Liliana Morales, a Cuban immigrant among many others, seeking her share of the American dream. This woman has been locked up in Manhattan's Bellevue Hospital since her arrest, so how did this piece of cardboard land in my mailbox? The most insane hypotheses and disaster movies are spinning in my head on a loop.

Who helped her get the card out of the hospital?

I'm appalled. The psychiatric department of Bellevue Hospital is the oldest, most renowned and safest in the country, but malfunctions can occur. Liliana Morales is not in a resort, she's detained, restrained, handcuffed when necessary, and kept in a high security section of the prison. I know the grounds because I visited the facility during a coverage about the prison accommodation of the mentally ill. The procedures and regulations of this department are extremely restrictive. Not really the perfect spot for a vacation. Moreover, her criminal history and the cruelty of her murders have made Liliana a closely watched prisoner.

I hope they haven't loosened their surveillance; she'd be willing to do anything...

Eventually, amidst my walk up Madison, I turn back around. A few minutes later, I'm window-shopping in front of the Beretta store again, wedged between a clothing shop and a high-end jewelry. My move is against my convictions, motivated by an anxiety that has my stomach in knots. I try to convince myself that I am balanced enough to own a gun, which is an absolute illusion, but I need the decoy to walk right over my convictions, to walk through the door. Coming to the banal but effective conclusion that I'd rather be the shooter than the victim, I, Spencer Hogg, a convinced pacifist, push open the thick, bulletproof glass door of the largest arms supplier of the world's most armed democracy.

There is a lot of light in the store, the steel shines behind the armored showcases. The salesman is a woman, much to today's trend, like a revolver in feminine hands would seem less dangerous. My request makes her smile – she has few revolvers and Virginie, from the name embroidered on her jacket, explains with a smile that could melt icebergs that a pistol is much smaller, more practical and easier to handle than a Colt 45 or 38 special. Easier to load too. I'd be okay with any but I'm not a connoisseur and she sees it right through me, pinning a gun in my hands.

"It's a Px4 Storm, the latest model. It's sold with several interchangeable stocks: wood, metal, five colors."

I try and crack a joke. "Soon, you'll match the stocks to the color of your customers' eyes!"

She stares at me coolly. "I don't think we have that option, but considering the color of yours, we should!"

The she-devil smiles charmingly as I picture her as a Disney wicked fairy. I feel suddenly very alone in the store with this beautiful woman, my funny bone and a gun in my hand.

"Tell me, Virginie, it's not loaded, right?"

A confident smile creeps up her face. In sales, me calling her by her name means that everything is going smoothly and that she has a serious chance of closing the deal.

"No, it's not allowed inside the store."

She then asks me if I'm comfortable, probably seeing that I've never held a gun in my life. I handle it cautiously in front of the large mirror covering the entire back wall of the shop. The placement isn't random, cleverly positioned for customers to act bravado or assess if they'd look good with a gorgeous woman on their arm and a big gun in their hand. I get caught up in a game that is no longer one.

"How many bullets can the magazine fit?"

"In the nine millimeters option, you can choose between ten or twenty. The intermediates options need to be ordered."

11

"Really, twenty?"

"Yes. It's rare, but we have the option thanks to the New Jersey Police Department that made it a prerequisite for equipping its officers."

Pride shines in the young woman's eyes.

"If professionals have chosen it then it's settled! I'll take one but please no obvious box."

"It comes in a Beretta Waxwear, a city bag with two magazines and two boxes of ammunition. What would you like, the ten or the twenty magazine?"

I only hesitate for a second.

"Twenty!"

"You're right – it's safer, just in case."

I'm slowly getting used to being very stupid.

"Do you have a firearms license?"

"It's a little dated, but I do."

In fact, I've had it since the end of September 2001. Taking out my wallet and my credit cards, I hand her my ID. She makes a copy and gives it back to me, staring at me intensely for a few long seconds, sporting that special smile, hesitating between appreciation of her origin and assumed egotism of a saleswoman paid on commission. Virginie doesn't blink before offering me the generous gift of the house.

"We can engrave your name on the stock, or your initials if your name is too long, free of charge."

"Would Spencer Hogg fit?"

"Yes it would!"

"Just kidding, I'd rather not have my name on that thing."

"It's up to you."

Her smile had disappeared. She puts everything in a nice leather bag with the Beretta logo. I ask for the less noticeable one. She nods, bends her pretty body behind the counter and pulls out a huge, beach-style pouch with flashy American flag colors. She holds it out to me with her manicured fingertips and I shove the bag into the pouch before leaving.

With my purchase of the day under my arm and enough ammunition to support a siege rather than supporting my convictions, I flee in big strides the place where my brain surrendered. What has been done is done and I am not the kind of man to ever regret his bad decisions. I actually feel relieved in regards of Liliana Morales' threats, this gun tips the scale to my advantage.

I find myself in the crushing crowd again and I smile, reassured from walking around with a tool invented to kill. It makes me feel more alive, more powerful, more dangerous. The feeling is strange, but not unpleasant at all. Kind of like a confrontation with myself.

Are there armed men and women walking serenely, a Colt hanging from their belt, in this very crowd where I stand?

I now understand why the most lethal amendment of the Constitution has so many supporters. A regulated militia is necessary for the security of a free State – people's right to keep and bear arms must not be infringed. Amen!

God bless America! Yes, but which one?

I don't feel like getting worked up about the situation. I've always been against the sale of weapons but I just bought one. It's much easier to have beliefs than to stand by them.

As soon as I get back to the apartment, my phone rings. It's my psychiatrist. I have a smile that isn't really one, a gun in my beach bag and my psychiatrist on the other end of the line. What could be more normal in the world's greatest democracy?

2

"Spencer?"

"Yes, this is he."

"This is John Blatters, I'm calling from my office before I head to the hospital. Sorry to bother you."

My heart suddenly races. Blatters is also Liliana Morales' psychiatrist, and it's not a habit of his to call his patients.

"What's going on?"

"How can I put this... I'm afraid I don't have good news."

"Just tell me please."

"Do you remember Liliana Morales?"

"I don't see how I could have forgotten her. What did she do now?"

"I just got off the phone with the hospital director. She apparently did a lot of damage before she ran away from the psychiatric ward."

"Wait, back up. What do you mean?"

"She escaped. I don't have all the details yet except that she killed a nurse and someone from the cleaning staff."

I'm speechless, completely unable to speak.

"Spencer, are you still there?"

I feel like I've been hit on the head, having trouble recovering.

"For God's sake, doctor, she was in maximum security cell! What the hell happened?"

"I don't know much more, I just wanted to warn you."

"When did it happen?"

"We're not sure, probably late yesterday afternoon. I wanted to tell you right away: she's still very upset about her son's accident, specifically towards the person responsible for it."

"You know very well that I had nothing to do with it!"

"I do but she doesn't, and we can't tell her that without revealing your identity. Fortunately, she doesn't know you, and that's a good thing because her illness makes her extremely dangerous…"

My whole body twitches. "How the hell did she get away?"

"I have no idea yet but I'll let you know as soon as I do. I just wanted to give you a heads up."

"You really don't know much, doc. Do you realize that we have a public danger roaming the streets? A crazy criminal, capable of all kinds of bloodsheds!"

"Don't worry, we'll do everything in our power to find her as soon as possible."

"*Don't worry*? How can I not when I've received a threatening letter this morning!"

The doc is silent, slowly processing the info. After a beat, he asks in a disbelieving way: "A threatening letter? From whom, Morales?"

"Who else would threaten me?"

"How is it possible? Last week she was still complaining about not having been able to track you down."

"Well, it's very possible if the card I got this morning in my mailbox is to be trusted. Are you sure that she didn't go through your files at the hospital?"

"I'm sure, they're in a digital safe."

"You were the one who treated her at the beginning of her incarceration!"

"That's right, and I still am, but she never had access to any information about you. I see you in a private practice, not in a hospital ward. The files are kept separately."

"Then how does she know my name and address?"

"I don't know!"

"You guaranteed that she would never escape!"

16

"There had never been any escape from the psychiatric ward before!"

"And what a great first that is! What are you going to do about it?"

"Look, if she knows where you live, then it's more serious than I thought. I'll see if I can get you police protection."

"Don't overdo it, there's no need for that as long as I'm home. I live on the seventeenth floor, the elevator is code-protected and my door is bulletproof."

"I'm sorry, Spencer, but we'll have to keep that in mind until we find her and lock her up."

"We'll talk about it later."

"I'm telling you, Spencer, you'd better be careful with a neurotic madwoman like Liliana Morales. Very careful!"

"Is she really a psychopath? Are you sure of your diagnosis? Because when she was first arrested, the newspapers published anything and everything about her mental illness."

"Psychopath? That's a probability. But sociopath? This is guaranteed. Unfortunately, it might even be worse than that but I'll explain everything later. Stay home, don't go out. I'll come by as soon as I can."

"That's not very reassuring. Come quickly, I'll be waiting for you."

"I'll be by later, Spencer. I'll head to the hospital first before going to the police station. I might be there for a long time. I'm held liable and the Chief is taking this escape very seriously. The thought of having a crazy murderer on the loose doesn't really bode well!"

Blatters hangs up and I turn on the TV. The news channel broadcast the info in a loop, with old documents dating back to her incarceration, underlining the atrocious murders of the cleaning company's deliveryman and the nurse in charge of the criminal.

The afternoon is long. I call the hospital every hour to see if John Blatters is back, but I only manage to reach him at the end of the day. In a couple of words, he confirms what I've read on the Internet: sociopathy is a serious behavioral disorder, so extreme that resorting to crime can become a problem-solving method like any other. Right away, I feel like I've become some kind of wild game, a target in the line of fire.

He adds in a softer voice. "She's borderline too. I'll explain –"

"No, you're explaining it now!"

"In addition to her sociopathy, she's a twisted manipulator. It's extremely rare, but she is capable to show empathy to hook her victims and get her way."

"What does that mean exactly?"

"That it's easy for her to build a strong relationship with people if she has ulterior motives. If she fails though, if the victim refuses, she's capable of the worst because she can't control her impulses."

"She kills to get what she wants?"

"Yes, even if it's as a last resort. I remember one of her answers to a cognitive test: *as long as I can talk to people, I can manipulate them… Once I've gotten what I needed, it's over for them!*"

"Dr. Blatters, science has its limits and I find it difficult to imagine that madwomen can be sane!"

"This woman has above-average intelligence and a heightened sensitivity. She's wary of everyone and everything, and she becomes extremely paranoid in stressful situations."

"Okay, I'll believe you. But it doesn't help my case!"

After a beat, Blatters adds. "Although, there's one thing that we don't understand. Her irrational attachment to her son. This is not how this illness usually works."

"Even the craziest ones have a maternal instinct? I don't know if I should laugh or cry about it!"

"It's usually the opposite, they completely reject offspring, family, acquaintances, etc."

Shivers run through my body. "That's just great. What you're saying, doc, is that if I get in her way, she'll slaughter me."

"More or less. Knowing her, she won't just wait for fate to put you in her path, she'll bend fate to get to you."

"Lovely! Do you have other good news?"

"I'm sorry, Spencer, but you need to take the necessary steps to protect yourself. Keep in mind that Liliana is a killer, and she has a lot to be angry about."

"But I told you that I had nothing to do with it!"

"Except that you were in the wrong place, at the wrong time."

When I hang up, I can't stand still anymore and decide to go down to Kate's. I put on my jacket and rush down the seventeen floors by the back stairs. I don't want to take the elevator, to willingly put myself in a cage without knowing who will be behind the door when I get to the lobby. After thinking about it, I come to the conclusion that getting out two floors before my actual destination, whether going down or up, will ensure my safety.

The setting sun floods the entire avenue, the light invigorating me. I walk through the streets without any real goal other than keep moving. I turn around often to check that I'm not being followed. I regret not having taken the gun with me. I did hesitate but ended up leaving it in the open on the living room table. I have to ask my friend Archie, a Marines First Lieutenant, to show me how to use it. For now, Liliana Morales is hunted by all the police forces of the City and must be hiding somewhere, meaning that I shouldn't be much at risk – or that's what I'm trying to tell myself. It's fall, it's sunny and cold, and yellow cabs are stopped at a red light, smoke coming from the back, feeding the greenhouse gases. I raise my collar and walk faster.

I stop for a drink at Kate's, a remake of an Irish pub with shiny brass and warm, reassuring colors. Despite the ban, Kate is smoking her favorite cigars while the patrons are leaning on the bar, drawing on their cigarettes with impunity. The smoking cops often visit the place too and are always careful not to snitch on their last haven of freedom. Kate's pub is also the safe place of the port's customs officers. Here, you enter a closed universe where only the regulars feel comfortable. The selection is natural. Not wearing a uniform and being a journalist for *The New Yorker* should have been a big hindrance to my integration but Kate is a long-time friend, she was vocal about it, and nobody so much as throws me a sideway glance anymore. Needing comfort, I order a bourbon, neat. Kate pours it with a big smile, the one she keeps for her friends.

I can't help but ask my bar neighbor, a slouchy guy with a mustache, what kind of gun he wears on his belt. He turns to me, sizes me up, and looks at the owner before answering. She nods slightly.

He relaxes and replies with a proud smile. "A Glock 19, semi-automatic!"

"I thought you guys were all equipped with a Colt, the 38 special."

"No, not anymore."

"I'm sure I've seen some recently though."

"It's possible; some officers are still allowed to carry them. Old-timers who don't know anything but this gun."

"You learn something new every day. Next round's on me!"

"Thanks! Do you like guns?"

"No, not really. But I just bought a Beretta, so any info could be useful. There were more guns on the shelves of the shop than milk cartons in drugstores."

The cop starts to laugh. "You're right, there's a lot to choose from! Did you buy it from someone or on Madison?"

"On Madison."

"Rest assured, Berettas are good."

I hang out at the bar for a long time, talking, and I feel safe even if I don't fit in with these cops in uniform. Kate wants to talk to me; the news of the murder has spread. Everyone has their own version and we hear everything and its opposite, short of Liliana Morales devouring the corpse of her nurse before fleeing the scene.

Cuban immigrant, skin almost black, criminal fury... I understand that armed or not, she doesn't stand a chance of getting out alive if she crosses a cop's way: color blindness regarding criminals' skin shades is not too common in the New York Police Department.

I end up going home to watch the news. The freezing evening air feels good. All these hours have passed slowly and quickly at the same time. I pour myself a drink to get some warmth in my stomach but I don't touch the gun. The steel looks shinier, more hostile than in the store. I rest while the City, seventeen floors below, turns on its lights all the way to the Bronx.

I turn on the TV and Liliana Morales' face appears framed on the living room screen. The picture shows a young woman, with skin not so dark, an emaciated yet angelic face, and a dark, unnaturally piercing look. I jump up, like I've been bitten by a poisonous beast, grab the gun, point it at the face and fire five or six times, but the magazine is empty. I feel a morbid relief every time I pull the trigger. The gun isn't loaded, but I couldn't resist the impulse, more vengeful than defensive. But if my Beretta had been loaded and this woman had been in front of me, would I have pulled the trigger? I know at that moment that if she tried to break into my house, I'd shoot. I feel hatred invading me... And despite rationality, a strange, irresistible attraction for this woman capable of tricking her guards, fighting with her bare hands, and risking death to see her son again. I'm angry with myself for not hating her completely. She wants to kill me but I can't picture her as a mortal enemy. My

21

shrink will help me get to the bottom of this early, weird Stockholm syndrome. It was an uncomfortable feeling, kind of unintelligible and insane, like the hate you keep feeding to make sure that you really loved.

I lay there, not sleepy, feeling this woman pick at my brain, jumping at the slightest noise, hearing things I never heard before, and listening to my building live. I resisted the temptation to load the gun, I just put the magazine next to it on the coffee table. Better be safe than sorry.

It's amazing how the mind can self-suggest, invent a worst-case scenario, and put fear in your heart. It won't be easy to live with. I get up and make coffee in the kitchen, pouring a glassful of rum, enough to knock out an ox, and I swallow the whole thing down before going back to bed. I treat insomnia as I would do with heartbreak. I know it's effective, that the alcohol works, and I fall asleep with a sleep as heavy as the Beretta weighing on my stomach.

3

The night is short.

I wake up at 6 a.m. and take a cold shower to get my head in the right place before finishing the article on Fado. George, the *New Yorker* editor, also known as Jo and, for the luckiest ones, Jojo, calls to yell at me. He's been waiting for my column to complete the cultural edition of the week. I'd promised him a piece on Mariza, the Portuguese fadista diva, a woman I interviewed last week at Joe's Pub in New York City.

In the middle of the morning, after two cups of coffee, I call Jack Field, a special agent at the FBI. Gina, his wife, works for the cultural weekly *Time Out-NY* as a freelancer and I've helped her out a few times. In return, she assured me that her husband would be around in case I ever need him.

Jack is a Bureau agent like no other. His job is to search, snoop, and collect, more Peeping Tom than investigation journalist. The task has been huge since the Patriot Act, introduced on September 11th, 2001, which allowed the FBI to conduct investigations for all crimes, even small offenses. Jack has access to most, if not all, of the police websites and, as far as I know, he's the only guy who can give me information on the Morales case. We see each other from time to time but we're not really friends; we're good pals. I don't want to have to call him, to beg for information from people I don't consider as friends, because sooner or later they always make you pay.

My call surprises him, but my request surprises him even more. We start by making small talk before I dive into the serious stuff. Right off the batch, I know he's sensing that something's off. It could be his cop's intuition making him wary of why a journalist would be calling to gather info on the murderer of the day.

"Why are you interested in her?"

"Who isn't?"

"I hear you, but this is usually not up your alley. You don't do crimes."

"Yeah, I know, but I need to cover something fresher than my cultural columns, to write papers that are more in tune with what people are experiencing."

"Good God, Spencer, they fortunately rarely experience this!"

"Maybe they don't, but Morales' crime records have created one hell of a fear climate in the City, and the TV adds more to it with every newscast!"

I can feel he's still suspicious, not too inclined to tell me what he knows. We appreciate each other but he's not ready to take that step. It's not a strict refusal but a small distance that he creates before making his mind.

He continues. "She sure did succeed in scaring everyone, you'll be sick when you know the details."

"Really? That bad? You know, I've seen a lot of crap when I was a correspondent in Iraq."

"This is top barbarism." He suddenly changes his mind, sighs, coughs, and clears his throat. "All right, but you didn't talk to me, you only take the facts, and you leave out anything that can be traced back to me. And no logorrhea in the columns of your newspaper."

"You have my word. Don't worry, I've never betrayed my sources."

"I'll send you what I have by e-mail, and I'll cross out in red what shouldn't come out in the open."

"Right, I'll be careful. Thank you, I owe you one!"

"You do. Do you still have your cottage at Windham Mountain?"

The dude doesn't waste any time.

"Yes!"

"I'd like to spend a few days in the mountains. Could you fix me up?"

"No problem. Are you bringing Gina?"

He clears his throat again, sounding suddenly embarrassed, and I understand why he agreed to help me.

"No, she'll be working. I'll go with a colleague from the office."

"An impromptu seminar?"

"You've got it!"

There's a long pause. No need to be a West Point graduate to guess what will happen next. I'm not a prude or a righter of wrongs, but I'm pissed that he's associating me by design to this adulterous vaudevillian escapade. This is a step aside I could do without.

"Damn it, Jack, I know your wife. Can't you get a hotel?"

"Spencer, do you have any idea what a married FBI agent with three kids and a mortgage makes?"

"Cut the crap, you're probably about $70,000 a year!"

"Yeah, but a favor for a favor. Right?"

"This is more than a favor…"

"Maybe, but I don't have many friends who own a beautiful cottage two hours from Manhattan."

Friend… The title makes me smile, but I don't have a better source on Liliana Morales. In other words, I have no choice and Jack knows it. No wonder he was so quick to hand me his info on the Manhattan hitwoman. It doesn't cost him a dime and he solves a cash flow problem at the same time.

"All right. I'll call the agency that manages the cottage."

"I wouldn't expect nothing less from you!"

"Tell me, Jack, what if I had refused?"

"I'd have refused to give you the documents."

It's very clear now. I have to remember that I'm dealing with the best snoop cop in the New York office. This guy is the type to take rather than to give. And I don't want him, all new friend that he is, sticking his nose into the most recent events of my life.

"When do you feel like going?"

"Next weekend. The weather will be great, it'll be a nice change of scenery to be in the mountains, near the snow, and by the warmth of a fire."

A salacious image crosses my mind. "Forget the animal skin, I've got a hardwood and stone slab flooring."

"Too bad…"

His unusual laughter, a bit greasy, makes me uncomfortable. I get into the practicalities. "Don't forget to change the sheets, close the shutters, turn off the water and electricity."

"No worries, I will!"

"And don't you dare leave thongs or underwear around, I have a private life too!"

Actually, I was lying about my private life. Nothing had been going on for a long time in that department. Lindsay, my last girlfriend, had run off with my lawyer, not without having previously liquidated my savings plan to set up a clothing store in Manhattan. Since then, I'd hit the brakes on lovers twenty years younger than me, at least until I was restored to health financially.

A burger later, an email from Jack is sitting in my mailbox. I print the most important documents of the thick file, surprised by the profusion of information, and by their quality. These very personal secret notes exist for any human of this country; the NSA[2] and Facebook aren't the only ones that spy on the sly. The icing on the cake is that Miami police officers have recovered three notebooks full of intimate notes Liliana had been writing since she was a teenager during her first rampage on the American soil.

---

[2] The National Security Agency.

26

Upon reading the documents, I discover that she was born in the suburbs of Havana, Cuba, twenty-six years ago, and that her son, Mario, is almost eight. The math is simple: pregnant at seventeen or eighteen, doubly out of love. I pour myself a drink. Jack Field's notes are in the margins of the body of the text or on separate sheets. His writing is tight, almost unintelligible. I resume my reading.

"Like the vast majority of Cuban refugees, Liliana and her son arrived illegally by sea and were taken under the Cuban Adjustment Act, the association that protects its citizens as soon as they arrive in the United States and helps them write their application for permanent residence. While waiting for the precious paper, the mother and son found shelter via a charity with the Diaz family, Cuban cousins in the large Miami community."

Following are several pages on her history. Before landing on an American beach, I learn that Liliana had been under heavy treatment since her admission in the infamous psychiatric unit of the Havana hospital, where she had been placed to serve a six-year sentence. I sip my drink.

Sentenced to six years as a minor? I'm dealing with a real criminal.

She escaped four years before her time was up and, of course, the psychiatrists were concerned about her mental illness. I read at the bottom of a page *"Extremely dangerous"* written in red. No psychiatrist in his right mind would have dared to sign her release, even at the end of her sentence. It quickly becomes clear that it's difficult for the average folk to guess what her illness is. As long as no one gets in her way, she behaves almost normally and can hold a conversation flowingly. During her incarceration, her dementia strokes seem to have spaced out thanks to shock treatments at the hospital, and the doctors were hoping to stabilize her. After her escape, though, and without proper care, she may have become terribly unstable.

A dated history follows. Her sociopathy had bloomed in her teens – it's usually the case for patients like her – following heavy traumas that piled during her childhood.

27

The consequences had altered her judgment, weighing heavily on a brain that's neurotic to the core.

Whether you take these psychic and physical damages as cause or consequence, Liliana's story has been a long succession of tragedies and violence, like underprivileged families often experience. The poor, wretched families of the slums of the great port of Havana are no exception.

The death of her mother, Dora, when Liliana was twelve, because of poorly treated meningitis that hadn't been properly diagnosed, triggered her first signs of madness. It was on that date that the Havana psychiatrists had dated the beginning of her illness, severe sociopathy, probably coupled with latent dementia. After her mother's death, Liliana was left alone with Ernesto, her father, who was a very strong man physically, but with a weak, easily influenced mind. A man without any real culture, except the one of the streets, that didn't have a real job and was barely getting by. Half rogue, overpowered by his wife Dora, whom he loved with all his heart. She was the one who put food in their stomachs and who brought money home; her disappearance left him drained with empty pockets, and the problems of a daughter he was unable to raise. He sought comfort in alcohol, rum, odd jobs, schemes, scams, gambling, and cockfights, spending the few dollars he earned poorly and going from poor to very poor. In his misery, he became irritable, perverse, lost what little dignity he had left, and let the unrepairable happen.

As always, it took a combination of circumstances to drag the father and the daughter into a nameless abyss.

4

At that time, Ernesto was regularly questioned by the Cuban police officers about the violence and fights he was familiar with. The notes and minutes were all overlapping. It was the day before a weekend, and he'd just come back from a cockfight very drunk where he had bet his last pesos. He was furious and frustrated to not have had enough money to pay Carla, his usual prostitute, who had sent him away bluntly.

"Come back when you have enough money!"

"I'll pay you tomorrow, I swear!"

"Then you'll fuck me tomorrow!"

"Bitch!"

"That, Ernesto, I already knew but be careful of what you say. I don't have Dora's patience, may she rest in peace!"

Ernesto had swallowed his rage and had gone home. Alcohol always made him mean, but mixed with sexual frustration, the cocktail had been explosive that night. He wasn't a bad guy, but between a childhood spent in the terrible orphanages of the island and his lack of guidance since his wife had died, the balance was tilting dangerously on the wrong side.

It was late and Liliana was sleeping in their shared bedroom. Without money to afford clothes, she had to put on her mother's nightie, her dresses, her underwear, and her shoes. Ernesto stayed a moment in front of his sleeping daughter without touching her. He just looked at her, rocking on the balls of his feet. He felt his sex harden, and, in his frustrated and drunk mind, the body of his late wife mixed with his daughter's – at least that's what he tried to believe, without luck.

To push away his impure thoughts, he threw himself on his knees before the large crucifix hanging on the wall and begged

God to take away his incestuous thoughts. When he got up, his desire was stronger than ever but he'd promised himself not to touch Liliana. He leaned over and kissed her in her sleep, as he did every night. His daughter's smell, so similar to his wife's, and the heat made his resolutions crumble. Letting himself fall on the bed, he crushed Liliana under his weight.

He felt her twitch, trying to free herself, and it excited him even more. He held her head on the pillow, rolled the nightie up, lowered his briefs that were too large but still acted as protection, and penetrated her brutally. His pleasure was immediate, brutal, and almost painful, like a dam that gave way. Too drunk to hear his conscience, he collapsed beside his victim and fell into a dreamless sleep.

Liliana hadn't shouted. She was a virgin, but not that innocent: her mother had explained some things to her while the television, the social media, the girls in the street and the magazines had taught her the rest. It was the weight of her father slumped on top of her that had woken her up. She knew that it was him, which is why she hadn't screamed when she had felt the hardness of his sex brutally clear a way inside her, tearing her kidneys. She was stunned by her absence of reaction, by her indifference despite the pain, her immense fury, and her disgust. She couldn't know that this indifference to her fate, that this cold and impersonal way of reasoning, were the signs of the first spike of the illness.

She fell asleep and got up at dawn, as usual, to heat some water and clean herself from the blood that was soiling her thighs. Ernesto, with his pants still around his ankles, was snoring. She looked at him, the pot of boiling water in her hand, hesitating, thinking that an accident could happen quickly. It only would take a small clumsy wrist twist to get revenge, but she ended up emptying the water into a bucket and washing herself.

She didn't try to understand. Despite the aggression, her dad was the only family she had left and her only protector against the other men in the neighborhood.

When, after a long sleep apnea, he woke up and got up, she didn't blame him, going about her business as if nothing had happened. She told herself that she was now playing the role of her mother to feel less guilty. Ernesto didn't understand and didn't try to find out why his daughter was so willing to be raped. He blamed it on her innocence, and then, to clear his conscience, thought that maybe she liked it. He stopped praying but continued drinking, and Liliana had to continue accepting her father's abuse when he didn't have enough money to afford Carla, his favorite whore.

The girl grew up without rebelling but with an ever-growing hatred of her father, but never giving in to the furious desire to kill him that what rising inside her like a powerful wave, wanting to avenge the paternal incest. She withdrew into herself, kept her rage, and resisted the impulses that the illness was submitting to her brain.

On her seventeenth birthday, she was drafted into the Revolutionary Armed Forces like most young Cubans who didn't attend school. Cuba needed exceptional soldiers to ward off American vindictiveness. She was quickly spotted for her intelligence and fighting skills, and was taught to handle weapons and explosives, to mine and clear mines, to fend for herself in a hostile environment, and to kill with knives or her bare hands. She felt no fear when facing danger and never gave in to panic. Her self-control and her cold blood were signs of the dangerous neurosis that invaded her more each day.

Cunningly, she gave in to the advances of her superior, Sylvio, a frustrated, rather ugly, and sickly jealous NCO who saw in her the opportunity to satisfy his macho and overflowing sexuality. He believed her to be a virgin and took pride in depriving her of her virginity, taking her in a way he'd never been able to take any woman. She let him just like she has let her father: without any emotion. Sylvio, thanks to his rank, was useful in freeing herself from a heavy social status and helped her forget where she came from.

But Sylvio made the mistake of falling quickly in love with Liliana, believing to be the dominant male in the couple. Perfidiously, she encouraged his fantasies, let him abuse her when and as he wanted, until the day she refused. Too in love and, dominated rather than dominating, he didn't force her. After a few days, without even noticing it, he'd become an obedient puppet.

It lasted for six months, until the fateful day when he returned early from a military operation and found her in bed with a lieutenant from his own regiment. In a rage fit, he tried to push the lovebirds out of the window but ended up almost falling over, becoming the laughing stock of a regiment of men that didn't accept a ridiculed leader. The commander asked him to apply for a transfer or to be prepared to be fired.

Humiliated as Latinos can be when their virility is impaired, he ruminated on his revenge until, one night, he drugged Liliana before handing her over naked, blindfolded, and with her wrists tied to five violent reservists who were visiting the barracks. Drunk, excited by the opportunity, aware of their impunity, and stunned by the beauty of the prey their superior offered them, they raped her shamelessly.

Liliana never knew the names of the men who had forced her that night. She was resentful, kept a rage-crushing heart and, so that she wouldn't forget, a child within her bruised womb. This time again, she resisted the impulse to kill, but she promised herself that she would avenge herself for what Sylvio had done to her. When Liliana first joined the military, she was a fragile and very unstable young woman. When she was released from service two months later, she'd turned into a trained, tattooed fury, terribly traumatized by the ultimate rape she experienced straight from the Army's forces.

Her father, Ernesto, was still living his pitiful life, deprived of his daughter but finally showing somewhat remorse. Always drunk, his health was deteriorating rapidly. He spent winter and spring drinking, smoking, gambling the little money he earned, and robbing his buddies to fuck Carla. Time passed without his daughter ever visiting him when she was on leave. It affected Ernesto, but he didn't go see her at the La Plata barracks, although it was only a few kilometers from his home. He waited patiently for her to finish her time. Perhaps then he would have the courage to see her again and ask for forgiveness for his terrible crimes.

Fate decided otherwise.

Shortly before Liliana finished her service, Ernesto, who was a brawler when he drank, got the shorter end of the stick in an early-morning fight, coming out of a clandestine gambling joint on the docks of Marimelena, one of the most notorious ports in Havana. His opponent's baseball bat hit him in the back of the neck, breaking the first cervical vertebra – the atlas – the one that carries the weight of the skull. He spent many months in the hospital and was properly cared for: Cuba knows how to take care of its citizens, whether poor or rich, without it costing them a single peso. Liliana didn't go to see him, even when she got out of the military. The doctors, as excellent as they were, brought Ernesto home five months later, paraplegic and in a wheelchair.

Liliana, who was seven months pregnant by then, didn't let him in. As soon as he got out of the ambulance, she wordlessly grabbed the handles and pushed the wheelchair in front of her without really knowing where she was going. Her father protested, but there was no response. She walked through the neighborhoods to the port, to the huge cement parapet called the Malecón that protects the city from the sea, and runs to the last spurs of Vedado. Ernesto didn't understand why she was taking him to the port instead of bringing him home. Finally, she stopped the chair at the top of the parapet that overlooked the ocean, near the tower at the entrance of the port. It was dangerously close to the shore, and Ernesto got angry.

"What do you want? Why are you bringing me here?"

There was no answer, only the wind picking up.

"I'm cold, cover me up!"

He became angry and demanded an explanation, sensing that something was wrong. His daughter was no longer the same: he didn't recognize the frail girl that had left him to serve his country. She'd become a muscular, feline woman with a visible pregnancy.

He questioned her again. "Why are we here? Are you expecting someone? Take me home, I'm cold!"

He waited before asking her in a fatherly tone. "Are you pregnant?"

This time, Liliana answered. She took a deep breath. "It's not yours."

There was a long silence, the wind intensified, and Ernesto began to pray aloud.

Sitting at the foot of the wheelchair, she waited for nightfall. Then she stood up, breathed in the sea air, and tightened the belt that held her father in an upright position, before whispering in his ear.

"Ernesto," she insisted on the word, having never called him by his first name. "Ernesto, do you remember the nights you forgot you were my father?"

He jerked in his chair and pulled on the belt to unhook it but, weakened by his long months of hospitalization, he only managed to bring his chair closer to the edge of the wall.

Liliana just had to push him with her foot. Ernesto screamed as he fell into the ocean. She watched the chair float before sinking into the water. Her father's cries of distress did nothing to her, even when a huge eddy on the surface signaled that the sharks that swarmed toward the harbor's sewage outlets were leaving a few teeth on the metal. Liliana, with her eyes staring at the water, didn't have an ounce of remorse when she saw the sea getting agitated, turning red.

She returned home, an unknown taste in her mouth and her soul soothed.

The scene hadn't gone unnoticed. A patrol of policemen, intrigued by the presence of a young woman and a cripple in a wheelchair near the cliff, had seen it all. That same evening, Liliana was sleeping in a cell.

Only one of Ernesto's arms was found thanks to a tattoo making it possible to identify him, a souvenir of his own military service. The criminal was twenty years old, about to give birth, and had no record. Her lawyer pleaded accident first, then manslaughter, and finally insanity after psychiatric examinations uncovered her mental illness.

She gave birth to a son, Mario, during an expeditious Cuban-style trial. Held responsible for her actions, she was sentenced to six years behind bars. She did one with her son in the Presidio Modelo prison on the island of Pinos, the infamous building, before being incarcerated in Havana's psychiatric hospital without Mario, as the institution didn't accept the kids of the sick. Because of the gang rape, Liliana didn't know who Mario's father was: a heavy mystery that she could never solve, but which left room for a paternal fantasy that she created to better love her child. She'd become deeply attached to this fatherless son that remained her only protection in a merciless prison population when it comes to parricides. And when, after a year, she had to hand him to the administration as the law required, when two women that looked like Cerberuses with sweet words tore him from her arms, she promised herself to come back, take him away from his jailers, and leave the island for good.

She missed Mario terribly.

It was her daily obsession, and she never stopped trying to get him back. She escaped a few months later during an authorized outing to the office of a greedy gynecologist who wanted to examine her without putting on gloves first. It was quickly settled. She nailed the hand of the doctor between her open thighs on the table with a scalpel, a short sharp dagger, before jumping from the second floor and running away. Then began a long run, the terribly nervous and neurotic young woman hiding in the outskirts of the port, in areas where the police hesitated to go astray. She looked for her ex-lover Sylvio, the NCO who, fired for yet another affair of morals, was slowly rotting away doing small-time security jobs. Ecstatic to see her again, he took her under his wing and promised to get her son back. She sold her body to eat, get dressed and pay the rent – there wasn't anything shocking about that. The jinetera is part of Cuban life and it's often the only way to survive. Before the revolution, pleasure girls were banned from society but things had changed and it was no longer shameful for a girl to be a jinetera. She brought the money that an honest activity in the slums of Havana was unable to produce.

Liliana accepted this whore job without batting an eye and without really being able to refuse. Sylvio forcibly recovered his son from the orphanage but, far from giving him back to his mother, used him as a hostage. It was common for pimps to use children to force their mothers to work. To get more money, he forced Liliana to work as a prostitute in a clandestine sex house. Forced to endure the daily assaults of horny males, she decided to flee Cuba. She didn't have much trouble seducing one of the brothel's regulars, a sailor who dreamed of getting his hands on a whore of his own and who already saw himself with a cigar on his lips and two-tones shoes on his feet. He recovered Mario and took him to a safe place. Liliana, finally relieved about her son's fate, fled the brothel but left enough clues for Sylvio to find her.

That was the last time he was seen walking, and he was soon found dying on the beach from stab wounds with his sex in his mouth. He owed his life to a squad of firemen and their daily jog. It was the second time that Liliana gave in to her illness. The brave sailor, frightened, was smart enough not to interfere any longer in the killer's life and disappeared into the wild, taking his amateur pimping dreams with him.

Despite the hunt, Liliana remained untraceable, for good reason. That same night, after having stabbed, stripped, and asked her son to turn around, she emasculated the man who had raped her before embarking on the semi-rigid of a smuggler for a large fee.

The sea was beautiful, calm as she arrived at dawn on a moonless night near the American coasts. The multitude of street lamps in Miami Beach sparkled in the sea. The ferryman pointed with his chin to a telephone booth's lights on the top of the longest beach in Key West. With a reassuring smile, he gave her three fifty-cent coins.

"This is the only coin-operated booth on the coast. Go make a call while I unload your stuff."

With her son in her arms, she jumped out of the canoe, holding the mooring line so she wouldn't fall, walking on American soil with water up to her thighs. She was only ten steps in when she heard the ferryman put the boat in gear and the engine roar. She turned around and saw the boat back up. Putting her son down on the sand, she ran into the waves and managed to grab onto the mooring line that was dragging in the water. The ferryman fired the engine and the boat pulled her more than three hundred feet before she had to let go. She swallowed water, nearly drowned, and was almost torn apart by the propeller when the man turned the boat around, heading out to the sea. Weighed down by her soaked winter clothes, Liliana struggled to reach the beach while Mario, terrorized by his mother's departure, had rushed to follow her. In the surf up to his chest, he lost his footing but she grabbed his arm before collapsing on all fours on the sand. She took her child in her arms and watched the boat disappear with her two suitcases and the bag with her ID, jewelry, and savings. She opened the hand she'd kept clenched hard enough for her fingernails to dug into her palm, and in the hollow, saw the unfortunate three fifty-cent coins shining under the stars.

At the top of the beach, in the harsh light of a phone booth visible for miles around, her heart pounding, her son clinging to her soaked clothes, her fingers shaking, she slipped the first coin into the telephone's slot and dialed immigration as she'd been told to do. Three rings were heard before an answering machine went off.

Hello, our offices are open every day from 10 a.m. to 6 p.m. Please call back.

5

Liliana arrived in town in the early morning. She looked pale, her wet clothes wrinkled and dirty, and her son's not much better. Her only luggage was a Miami address, the name of a restaurant run by her cousin, Fernando Diaz, a kid of her late mother's brother. This should be, at least she hoped, the first stop before reaching Pepita, the youngest sister who held a fast-food restaurant at the Brunswick crossroad in Brooklyn. She'd never seen either of them since their family had left Cuba before she was born, right before Fidel Castro came to power, and hadn't been back.

Liliana didn't lose her cool and asked a passerby walking her dog for directions. An hour later, exhausted but alive, she found herself in Little Havana, one of West Miami's three most dangerous neighborhoods. The kind of place where you shouldn't hang out after dark unless you want to lose your purse, your life, or both. Liliana knew the reputation of this predominantly Cuban neighborhood where speaking Spanish was the number one tacit rule. In the early hours of the Castro revolution, the bourgeoisie and political opponents had fled here massively, running away from the terror of executions without trial. The regime's survivors who stayed on the island all had a family member, a brother, an uncle, an aunt, or a cousin living in Miami or Orlando.

The big island was only a few hundred kilometers from the Florida coast and regularly poured its migrants onto the beaches, increasing the Cuban diaspora daily. In addition to the hope of a more peaceful life, there were many temptations in the land of the American dream.

Temptations that the Medellin cartel boss mob, Pablo Escobar, had known how to take advantage of. Pablo was the kind of killer that would make Liliana Morales look like a saint. But the drugs kingpin had an abrupt end when he was shot by the military, helped by American intelligence services. After a long hunt, Pablo died trying to flee his last hideout via the neighboring roofs. The bullet had barely grazed his skin that the Colombian cartel of Cali, led by the Rodriguezes, had taken over. The two brothers changed the game by offering cheap cocaine and a high-paying street job to all Hispanics in Miami, cops included.

The Hispanic community alone filled the 400 blocks of Little Havana and had the men and connections to set up a structure capable of moving tons of cheap crack. Many were called, and many were chosen. Under the Rodriguezes' orders, they set up the largest cocaine traffic ever managed, dealing several billion dollars every year. The drugs came in by the ton, and so did the money, forcing the cartels to store bills of ten and twenty on pallets in huge warehouses. The money was impossible to spend, useless, and at stake until lawyers got involved.

At that time, there was no law in the United States against money laundering. You could deposit mountains of cash in U.S. banks without the cashiers caring about their source, too happy to take their commission in the process. All the Cubans had to do was transfer the money to the cartels. Simple, but fraught with insecurity, paperwork, and fraud – even the crooks weren't immune to theft.

This legal void soon became a highway for crime, the thugs having a field day. However, the business got less interesting when a law severely punishing money laundering was passed. The drug money began to pile up again in warehouses without being spent. But a lawyer called Umberto Aguilar, smarter than most, found a loophole. He advised the Colombians to legally buy all kinds of businesses and industries in their home country, which allowed them to send the profits to shell companies in the United States via loans and investments.

40

This is how Miami became the most economically dynamic city in the United States. The money that was recycled came back into the pockets of the drug lords, closing the circle effectively.

Everyone benefited from the system. The money flowed so freely that the gringos, the Americans, flocked to take part in the El Dorado.

That was until the amount of drugs imported from Colombian labs by trucks, boats, and planes increased exponentially, the price per gram dropping by half. To restore their margins, Colombians physically attacked the competition of smaller cartels. Griselda Blanco, a native of Medellin, was the chief enforcer in Miami. Griselda was a tiny, ugly, unscrupulous woman and a proven psychopath with one goal: to clean up the mess. The result was six hundred dead bodies in the first year, including the all-too-famous Dead Land massacre, a pointless mass murder in the middle of a shopping mall in the suburbs of Miami, amidst tapas and a beautiful spring day.

The mayor, shocked to see his city burn up in flames, asked for help from the United States government. It took President Reagan, then in office, to send in the cavalry to restore calm. Federal agents got to work. A good decade was necessary to dismantle the cartels and stem the flow of cheap crack, proving that the Mafia was deeply rooted in the city.

Fernando Diaz, Liliana's Cuban cousin, ran a restaurant in Little Havana; but underneath his honest front, he was laundering dirty money. Former smuggler, he had started out piloting one of the huge speedboats for the Cali cartel, picking up coke packages thrown out of planes chartered by the drug traffickers. Fernando hauled them back to one of Miami's many marinas. He was responsible for every kilo of coke that was caught and had no room for error: he knew how dangerous the cartels and this area were. When Liliana had called him to announce her arrival, he'd warned her: Little Havana was not a peaceful haven for a young mother and her child.

"What kind of job are you looking for? Waitressing, something like that?"

"That would be a good start. I have a son to feed."

"I'll find you something but as Cuban as you are, you'll have to be very careful with your relationships. It's survival of the fittest down here."

"I'm not afraid."

"You should be. In this neighborhood, you can be robbed at any time or raped if you're worth it, and the attacker will shoot you dead without the slightest hesitation so you won't snitch to the cops."

He wasn't wrong.

I quickly understood from Jack's next note why he wasn't. When the imbecility of law generates, the day after its promulgation, borderline behaviors, you've got to wonder who this law really protects. The cartels' stranglehold on the region had pushed the authorities, alarmed by delinquency that had become endemic, to massively recruit agents and policemen to put a stop to the drug lords' business. In order to do the right thing, Florida passed repressive laws that were far too severe without worrying about their perverse effects.

The prison sentence for armed robbery got raised from five to fifteen, or often twenty years behind bars. The drugs traffickers quickly found a way to continue their business by reducing the risk of spending their lives in prison: police officers or not, they erased every evidence with a gun. Even if it was a step backward because most of the people who deal, kill or rape get caught sooner or later. And when the murdering drug traffickers have handcuffs on their wrists, a chain between their ankles, and a murder charge on their backs, no one erases anything anymore. With luck and an excellent lawyer, the maximum is life or, for dark skins and even darker records, capital punishment.

Statistics ended up soaring and the risk of being shot in the land of cowboys got twenty or thirty times higher than in the old continent... Everything's greater in America!

Liliana, soaked and missing a purse, was holding her son's hand tightly as they were keeping close to the walls. She went directly to Fernando's, the restaurant, where she was welcomed like a cousin. Dried, dressed, shod, and fed, she handed Mario to him and, the next day, was on her way to the immigration office to register her existence under a false identity, swearing that she had lost her ID during the crossing. This was the only way to get under the very special Cuban adjustment of status law. She knew that the Cuban police didn't give U.S. law enforcement information about their nationals. Gringos didn't have good press in the big island's administrations.

Within a week, her new family found her a position as a linen maid in a five-star residence. Her youth and beauty instilled trust. It wasn't a panacea, but she was able to learn what living in the USA meant. Taken to the bar of the neighboring hotel by a fellow citizen, she learned to wait at the local parties before Fabio, a Cuban who wasn't very popular here, spotted her and offered her work, food, and accommodation. This is exactly what she had come to Miami for: security for herself and her son.

Since she'd given up all treatment, her neuroses wouldn't let her rest. She hid her anxiety attacks and treated herself with other kinds of drugs. Her only source of happiness was loving her boy with all her might in a sick, excessive way. It was also when her cocaine addiction began, both due to the migraines that plagued her and to the bad encounters that a pretty woman without real resources couldn't avoid in the trendy bars of Miami.

It was in one of these places that she'd met Fabio, a half-pimp half-thug Cuban, a small-time hustler who made the mistake of seeing an easy prey in this young woman. He took her in and provided her with her first line of coke to help overcome the lack of pills, also providing her first clients to overcome her recurring need for money. That's how she started a whorehouse on Washington Avenue to buy her daily drugs and all that her beloved Mario needed. Fabio, like any good street teacher, left her alone for a few months before tightening the screw. She had to keep in line and make more money to recoup his initial investment. He put pressure on her by accusing her of spending too much time with her son and spending too much in general. But Liliana resisted. One evening, deciding to go up a notch, he went to her house just before dinner, and, as he'd planned, the argument escalated quickly.

"Did you work today?"

She didn't answer.

"How much did you make?" barked Fabio.

She tried to lie because she didn't want Mario, who was in her room, to hear the conversation.

"I don't know, I haven't counted yet. I'll do better tomorrow."

Fabio didn't mind, it wasn't the first time he had to straighten a woman out. He calmly slapped her once, then twice, and Liliana collapsed without a cry in a corner of the kitchen. With a confident smile on his face indicating that he liked hitting women, Fabio lifted Liliana by the hair and insulted her before dragging her on the floor and kicking her stomach, the spot where it hurts so much that you can't help but scream. Liliana twisted under the pain, shouted the cry that her torturer wanted; a scream that her son also heard. When the boy came running into the kitchen, Fabio slapped him too. Hard. The boy, stunned, fell against the fridge, his head hitting the door as he fell heavily to the ground.

Fabio shouldn't have hurt Liliana's flesh. A fuse broke in the mother's brain. The sight of her son, lying motionless on the tiles, his head strangely leaning against the fridge door, made her hysterical. She stood up, her back bent, her head down, ready for more hits, and grabbed the hot lid of the heavy cast-iron bowl where the "ajiaco", a traditional Cuban black bean stew, had been simmering for several hours. The blow that she brought with all her strength on Fabio's plexus burned and winded him. He opened his mouth to scream, but a second blow from the edge of the lid burst his front teeth and broke his jaw. His legs buckled and he fell to his knees. Liliana raised her lid one last time and brought it down screaming on his head in a closing-pot motion. Under the blow, Fabio's exorbitant eyes turned grey as he staggered for a short moment, and collapsed in his own pool of blood. Liliana threw the lid over the moans of her attacker and rushed to her son, who was slowly coming back to him. She pressed a cold tissue on his cheek, took him in her arms, and carried him to her bed, humming the lullaby she sang to him every night when she put him to sleep.

Later that evening, suitcases packed quickly since they didn't have much to begin with, the mother and the son took off hand in hand, leaving Fabio for dead and spitting on his body. They took the first flight out to New York City and landed at Pepita's, the Diaz cousin in Brooklyn.

Family wasn't so bad after all.

6

Fabio survived but was handicapped for the rest of his life. His jaw was badly reconnected, held together by pins, making him suffer and preventing him from eating properly. The Miami police, without any proof of his pimping activity, let him walk away and launched a search warrant for the fugitive – but Fabio didn't know her real identity. A young Cuban woman named Liliana, who just arrived: that's all he gave to the investigators. The DNA of the spit didn't have any match since she wasn't registered in the database. But in reality, the cops couldn't care less about a pimp and a prostitute. They were sure of two things: she had either run away from the United States and it was no longer their responsibility, or she had stayed there and would reappear one day.

They weren't wrong. In Brooklyn, Liliana went straight back to what she knew, to discreet prostitution. Her cousin Pepita put her up in a nasty studio in the backyard of the Brunswick fast-food joint that belonged to the neighborhood's kingpin. Pepita, the girlfriend of said mafia boss, managed the bar. Through the network of the gang leader, Liliana quickly got a fake ID and was able to work in the bar in the mornings, work the streets in the afternoon and register her son in a school that wasn't too regarding about parents' situation.

As time passed, Liliana, began to spoil Mario in a way she'd never been spoiled. She bought his love by getting him everything he wanted, giving in to all his whims with the money made by her p.m. job. Her gig at the bar was only meant to pay for their food and rent.

Liliana's latest gift was a state-of-the-art skateboard that Mario, a gliding fan, had asked for before some overzealous immigration cops took her away to check her identity. She'd been stupidly tricked by a frustrated customer who had called the services. Between her past, her fingerprints, her DNA found at the Miami apartment, and her fake ID, she went straight to jail, got trialed for assault and battery on Fabio, and was sentenced to three years in prison – two of them on parole. Fabio, on the other hand, got trialed for aggravated pimping, sexual assault, and assault and battery on a minor. He got sentenced to twelve years for both charges and was taken to Rickers, the Alcatraz of the East Coast, the prison island in the East River on the Bronx side, just a few blocks away from his ex-lover's cell.

In this very own antechamber of hell, his crooked face and victimized pimp story didn't really fit in. A pimp who doesn't know how to be respected isn't esteemed so he had to lay low and look down before the kingpin of his section. Fabio, like most of these people, despised women, or, more precisely, the weakness of the women or men he met. In prison, cowardice didn't disappoint – there was a strong competition in that area – and he quickly found his bodysuit. He kissed enough asses to get out of his section and join the GMDC (*George Motchan Detention Center*). The official in charge assigned him to a task that had been kept for this facility only: recovering and transporting the Big Apple's forgotten bodies, an ungrateful but rewarding job for a destitute prisoner. He had to help, along with a dozen other inmates, bury the anonymous bodies or those without family coming from the main morgue in New York City, before piling them in the mass graves of H. John Island.

Holding their breaths, getting their hands dirty, burying the bodies: none of it was a pleasant experience, but it was obviously not for this macabre task that Fabio had wanted to join the morticians. The team leader, Miguel, was a Cuban from Santiago, where Fabio was born. It was him who, after the death of one of the group's inmates, had insisted that Fabio joined the night shift.

48

Miguel had him swear to never say what he saw in exchange for a share of the profits. In the beginning, Fabio only had to cover his eyes and nose. This was not organ trafficking, but close to it. Miguel, the boss, used to be a veterinarian, was convicted of aggravated animal abuse. He performed surgeries without anesthesia on his clients' cats and dogs, whether they were sick or not, charging them full price. His cheapness had been his downfall. A customer had complained after an udder cancer surgery on her dog and, upon closer inspection, the dog wasn't sick in the slightest yet the veterinarian had removed her organs without putting her to sleep. In fact, not a single milligram of anesthetic was found in the dog's blood and all cancer tests came back negative. The dog had died of pain.

The case had horrified the public and the vet had been heavily sentenced. In prison, he exploited the corpses destined for mass graves, extracting dentures, gold or ceramic teeth, and rare metal prostheses before burying the bodies.

The work was done in the hold of the boat during the crossing. The guards preferred to stay away from the stench of the corpses, meaning the deck in the summer and sheltered near the pilot in the winter. Miguel had found a job worthy of his sadism, even if he'd have preferred alive bodies. Armed with pliers and scalpels, he extracted teeth and dentures, fractured femurs for prostheses, broke bones for titanium pins, and ripped open flesh to remove pacemakers. He groped the bodies and was unparalleled in his ability to feel under his expert fingers any abnormality due to a fracture. The scars told him exactly where to look.

A prison guard, corrupted to the bone, retrieved the bag at the end of the journey and sold it to the director of Bronx crematorium who had little regard for its origin, mixing it with his own production. The recycling was perfectly invisible.

Fabio, weakened by his head wounds, didn't last long; his companions of misfortune showed no mercy for his health problems. His jaw pins were making him suffer terribly and it was becoming increasingly difficult to eat. He asked his supervisor to return to a less harsh section but the administration refused. It wasn't up to the inmates to decide on their assignment and Fabio had to rot in corpses transportation for another year. Exhausted and terribly emaciated, he chose to betray his fellow inmates despite the risk and snitched in exchange for his reassignment.

The authorities took in the claim but decided against a scandal. They immediately shut down the mortuary shuttle and scattered the veterinary surgeon and his team in high-security prisons across the country. The prison director kept his word and reinstated Fabio in his former section, under a health pretense.

It didn't take long for the inmates to figure out who the snitch was. Snitches have a short life expectancy in prison and, one spring morning, Fabio was found hanging with his belt from one of his cell's window bars.

True suicide or helped suicide? No one wondered.

The case was closed.

Although convicted, Liliana turned her sentence around thanks to her lawyer who, expert after expert, argued self-defense and insanity at the time of the events. She was sent to the women's psychiatric ward and held on the fifth floor of the Bellevue Hospital Center in Manhattan. The doctors had quickly diagnosed her sociopathy and understood her dangerousness. They questioned the background of a woman who refused to share her name; she was Cuban, and that was their only lead. They asked their colleagues in Havana for pictures and fingerprints, just in case. Eventually, the doctors succeeded where the police had failed. The answer came quickly and Liliana Morales' formal wasn't long. They learned about the bloodstained pedigree of their patient, a mix of parricide and barbarism.

It was the chief physician of the neurological department, Professor Robert Midle, who was the first to take a look at the young woman's file. For this great professional, Liliana remained a psychiatric enigma. He didn't understand this emotional hold, this obsessive bond that she had with her son. Excessive affection didn't fit the usual symptoms of sociopaths, usually in complete denial of their feelings. He dismissed the dementia diagnosis of the Havana doctors and concluded that this was an extremely rare case of sociopathy with borderline tendencies. He agreed with John Blatters, whom he had entrusted the patient's care, but it wasn't enough. Something wasn't right. She was capable of killing without flinching to get her way or to fight for the only emotion she was feeling: her unconditional love for her son. But the diagnosis still didn't fit into any known box.

The medication and the talks stabilized Liliana. She suffered less from delirium, the crises spacing out. She was told that her illness could be cured, or at least lessened in intensity. It made her nod, asking on a loop when she could go out and see her son.

One gray, rainy morning, as she sat quietly in her barred-windows room, she received a letter from her cousin Pepita – who was raising Mario while she was away – telling her about the terrible accident that had happened to her son at the bottom of the Brunswick steep street. He'd been hit by a car while riding his skateboard. His spine was damaged and he was in an induced coma, on the verge of becoming a vegetable.

Worried sick, she asked to see her boy at Saint George's hospital. Considering her illness and her past, the administration refused. Liliana spiraled into a violent crisis, forcing John Blatters to straitjacket her before locking her up in a detention room with padded walls. A surveillance camera swept the whole room continuously, too high for a patient to reach, and the images were sent to the nurses' office. The young woman was foaming with rage, literally, and had to be put on high doses of neuroleptics. Three months of behavioral and cognitive therapy were necessary before she could be allowed to leave the room. Recovering quickly, she took advantage of the affection of Jane, an older nurse, to get out of the strict confinement. Liliana realized how attractive she was to Jane and soon, the "patient/nurse" relationship was reversed. It was Liliana's turn to listen to Jane, to understand her, to advise her, and to help her as she was experiencing a painful breakup with her partner.

Her partner was a woman, and Liliana had paid close attention to the information about the nurse's sexual orientation. She'd never seduced a woman before so this would be a first. Jane didn't realize the growing influence of her resident. Convinced of her good intentions, she pleaded for her protégée, forging reports so that they could walk together in the secure park of the hospital under her sole supervision.

A veteran of psychiatric hospitals, Liliana knew how security systems worked and knew their flaws. She also knew that without accessory, any escape attempt was doomed for failure. Jane would be the key to opening the doors of freedom. Every night, kneeling in front of a Christ hanging on a cross on her room's wall, she vowed to find the driver responsible for her son's accident and to kill him slowly. The supervisors thought she was praying and noted down her good behavior on the nightly logs.

Encouraged by Jane, Liliana began to attend Monday morning church services. The Mass was celebrated in a chapel built at the back of the park, which allowed her to learn about the blind spots of the cameras and to realize that, on Mondays, the rounds were less frequent and almost nonexistent when it rained too hard, due to a lack of guards. They preferred to stay warm behind the fogged-up windows. She memorized the comings and goings of the nursing staff as well as the habits of the suppliers who came from outside.

And that's where she found the flaw.

Every Monday, around noon, a driver came to deliver clean linen and to collect the dirty one from the previous week. When his work was done, he would back his old Ford up against the wall of the large laundry room and walk to the hospital canteen, where he would have lunch with his wife, who worked in the cleaning department. He usually locked his doors, but every other time, out of carelessness or laziness, he forgot.

Without the ignition key, it was impossible to steal the van, and if Liliana had that kind of skill anyway, she wouldn't have been able to get through the two security gates leading to the outside. But she didn't care, she was happy to have found a breach, even if she wasn't sure how she could use it yet.

While waiting to work out an escape route, she continued to get closer to Jane, who was increasingly responsive to her attentions. Day after day, Liliana stretched her net, put make-up on again, dressed sexier, with low-cuts, and started to reply to the timid moves of the nurse. She fueled Jane's desire, who saw in her a beautiful lost sheep she could bring back in the flock and, although her conscience was in the way, in her bed too.

Liliana leaned on Jane's arm during the weekly Monday morning walks, the only ones that were allowed. She faked being tired because of the drugs to push her body close to her quivering chaperone's.

The affair flared quickly.

Liliana gave in once and refused the following times. Jane became crazy with unsatisfied desire, yielding to the whims of her protégée. On the following Monday, the day of the service and the walk, a heavy storm had kept staff and patients within the hospital's wards. At the end of the Mass, Liliana convinced her chaperone to keep on walking even if Jane would have preferred to return to the intimacy of the room.

They walked arm in arm until 1:30 p.m., when lunch was over and the guards' attention impaired by their heavy stomach.

The rain had stopped and Liliana drew Jane towards the entrance of the cleaning room. The van was there, parked against the wall, waiting for the pending return of the deliveryman. The young woman pressed the handle of the side door: it was unlocked. She climbed into the van and, with a devastating smile, held out her hand to the nurse.

"Come on in, I want you!"

Fifteen minutes later, the driver sat behind the wheel. One more round trip and his day would be over. He turned on the ignition and the radio and got the car moving. As he approached the guards' station, he took out his badge, stuck it against the windshield, and slowed down. They rarely checked the service cars as long as the driver's face was familiar. Martin passed through the two security gates without a hitch. The guards waved at him as he passed, and he waved back with a broad smile. He liked this job, and he was happy about the pay too. *Unemployment is nothing more than a distant memory now*, he thought as he drove carefully down the avenue.

At the first red light, he hit the brakes and stopped the van. The sudden presence he felt behind him sent a rush of adrenaline through his veins but a belt tightened around his neck and began to choke him. He tried to free himself but Liliana had a strong hold. He unsuccessfully tried to catch his breath, his hands trying to grab the belt, clawing his murderer's, before his vertebrae gave away. The light had turned green. The killer put the warning lights on and the blocked cars passed the van with a honk. She went out the side door and quickly lost herself in the usual Manhattan sidewalk rush.

The police, alerted by the shopkeepers, arrived with sirens blaring. It didn't take a Ph.D. to understand how the driver had died. A tourniquet hung down his back, made of a leather belt and a wooden coat hanger. The man didn't have a fighting chance. Not a single one of the many cops thought that the killer could have been a woman. Liliana had learned from her army combat instructor to only stop when she heard the sound of cracking bone.

Hidden behind the bags of dirty laundry, the police found the naked, bloodied body of a woman. The nurse's eyes were wide open and a black thong was stuck in her mouth. Later, the coroner confirmed that she had been strangled with her own bra and that her tongue and left breast nipple had been bitten off. The murder caused a stir in Manhattan: a madwoman was on the loose in the streets of the city.

Out of habit, the media added to it. In professional fashion, they knew that horror was the best way, if not the most important one, to boost ratings, sales, and advertising rates.

7

Alone in my office, wedged on my chair, in this comfortable place where I've written so many articles, with a cup of hot coffee in my hand, I have only one question.

How did she find me?

I'm wondering who, besides John Blatters, my shrink, and Archie, my best friend, have heard about the secret linking me to Liliana. The doctor was bound by professional secrecy, and he probably didn't want me to blame him and his profession if he hadn't abided by his Hippocratic oath. As for the force of nature that was Archie, I've shared a lot of secrets with him. We've shared mine, his, and war secrets too heavy to carry. I know more about him than he knows about me.

Our bond had grown even closer when, after his repatriation as part of his PTSD therapy, he told me about his sniper missions in Afghanistan and Iraq.

"You need to know, Spencer, what I had to go through to survive and serve my country."

I'd listened to him, and it had soothed him to share what he'd been through, what he'd had to do to get through. I hadn't judged him. War wasn't pretty: people who fight always come out wounded and dirty. He had to turn to coke to survive, like so many other soldiers. The Middle Eastern plateaus are full of drugs, and war is less unbearable with a gram in each nostril. At first, he smoked. It was okay, but then his spotter got shot in the forehead and Archie came back to the camp with his brother's brains on his uniform. That's when he started to shoot heroin, thinking that getting high was a way like any other to forget. Months passed until that one morning, a little less coked than usual, he started shaking like he had Parkinson's. In order to keep up, he took a second dose and fell into a coma in the helicopter that was taking him to the operation ground. It was a good thing because it meant he could be transported faster to the hospital.

The doctors barely got him back. When he woke up, he was kindly asked to stop using if he didn't want to be a pension-less retiree.

He returned home without glory in a medical plane with the wounded of the massacre. The next day, after thorough examinations, he was put under the authority of a withdrawal rehab. A doctor helped him by feeding him buprenorphine morning and night; a name he'd remember all his life. Buprenorphine is Subutex's active molecule, the usual substitute for opioids and other opiate crap that ravaged the soldiers prone to depression or PTSD, no matter how tough they were.

The First Lieutenant hadn't escaped this fate: he might have been detoxified but post-traumatic stress quickly caught up with him. He came to see me after he'd been diagnosed and had started his new treatment, looking me in the eye like the childhood friends that we were, the kind you never quite leave.

"Well, Spencer, it's not original for a veteran like me, but my brain has gone rogue. It's infected by everything I witnessed there."

I didn't answer but hugged him.

He'd resumed, sitting on the big sofa in the living room. "I'm being medicated. Monitoring, therapy… I'm getting better. What I'm about to tell you is part of the therapy, if you're okay with that."

"Of course. You can tell me anything you want to, whenever you want to."

"Thanks, man. It'll be helpful that you used to be a war journalist – you'll understand without judging…"

We drank beers while he told me about his years as a sniper in the Marines. Hearing about gun heroes wasn't pretty but I understood, and I promised to him that I would stay with him as long as he needed to fully recover.

The sessions lasted three months, with him coming once a week, talking about what was bothering him, about his nightmares, but also about life in general with a coffee or a drink in hand.

One evening, he told me. "Spencer, I'm going to be reinstated in a psychology training service to help the soldiers coming back from deployment."

"You deserve it, and the people you'll help deserve you too."

"I'm happy to be back working, inactivity was weighing down on me. I'm ready! Well, there're still things to clarify first…"

"Like what?"

He scratched what little short hair he had on his head and replied in one breath. "It's about Sarah…"

"What about Sarah?"

"Do you think I can tell her what I experienced there?"

I didn't hesitate. "If you want my opinion, Archie, and I don't think I'm wrong, it's even highly recommended."

"I'm afraid she'll leave me if I tell her about all this crap!"

"Sarah's your wife, and she's not just any wife. She'll help you get through this."

"You believe that? It scares me."

"You? You're afraid?"

"Yes…"

He stared at me with his big pale blue eyes and I understood how much he loved his wife.

I answered with all conviction I could muster. "Trust her."

Archie and Sarah lived in a comfortable ground-floor apartment in the backyard of Spencer's neighboring building. The Army was paying him to speak with Marine units coming back from operation. It allowed him to be around his peers, to be useful to his country, and to prevent the after-effects he'd been through during active duty. As the years went by, the memories faded and his pain was greatly reduced. Archie was back to living again, sharing the life of a wife he worshipped.

The last time I heard about their future, there were even talks of having a child. Sarah, under her calm and composed appearance, had a fiery spirit. Not just any woman could put up with the life of a Marine Corps Lieutenant engaged seventy-five percent of the year in an uncertain, dangerous, and difficult to grasp battle.

"There are sailors' wives and then there are Marine wives," she often said with a big smile.

To this day, Archie still doesn't have a cell phone - the Army forbids him to use one. It's too easy to localize by malicious people so I don't really know how to reach him. When I call on the landline, Sarah answers.

"Hello, Sarah?"

"Spencer! It's good to hear you. How are you?"

"To be honest, I've been better. Do you know where I can reach your husband?"

"He's training in Washington – at least from what he told me."

"Do you know when he'll be back?"

"Tomorrow night, if he's done with the training."

"Tell him to come and see me please, it's important."

"You're scaring me. Is it serious?"

"I don't know, but I don't want it to be."

"As soon as he gets here, I'll have him call you."

"Thanks, Sarah, you're an angel."

I hear her laugh on the other end of the line, the laugh of a happy young woman. Sarah is indeed an angel. She's madly in love with her husband and he owes her a lot. Without her, it would have been incredibly difficult for Archie to get out of the slump where the war had taken him. Her sweetness, her intelligence, and her tenderness had weighed in the balance as much as therapy, Subutex included.

I wait for Archie to call or come up to the apartment to show him the threatening words, to tell him about the killer's intrusion into the building, and to find out if he spoke about the Brunswick's accident to anyone other than Sarah. He comes by at least once a week to share a burger, pizza, or to drink beers. It would mean a lot to see him; I know I can always count on him and his insight. It worries me to be in the dark. How did this woman get my address? How did she manage to stick that damn card in my box? I asked the janitor: he didn't see or notice anything. This woman may be insane, but she's a trained killer walking the streets in broad daylight while all the cops in Manhattan are dreaming of riddling her body with bullets.

Knowing where I live gives Liliana a good head start and I don't like it one bit. Not only is she openly declaring war, but she also knows where to have it; a weakness I find hard to bear. Especially since I have no idea where she might be hiding or how she plans to get to me. I doubt that she'll listen to the voice of reason. I wonder how to reach her, how to explain to her what really happened with Mario… Even if it's as simple as it gets.

I'm pouring myself a drink when the office phone rings with the first notes of Ó *Gente da minha Terra*, Amália Rodrigues' song covered by Mariza, the Portuguese diva. It's strange to hear this pure voice, these diamond shards in the middle of my anguish. Thinking about the Torre Bellem gardens concert calms me. Flashback to Lisbon, twenty thousand people shoulder to shoulder when, in the middle of the song, seized by emotion, we all stood up as one and applauded… She hid her tears while we let ours flow.

I wait before answering. It's not my usual behavior but I'm sure Liliana Morales will try to reach me, and, if she has my name and my address, she must have my number too. She's too angry with me not to give in to the temptation to pour out her hatred – she'll want to hear me scared. I'm no doctor, but I feel that in her sick mind she wants to terrorize me.

I pick up the phone.

"Hello."

It's Archie. I'm relieved yet strangely frustrated at the same time.

"Just in time. I need to see you!" I tell him from the get-go.

"Hello, Spencer."

"Yes, hello, Archie –"

"I know, I'm not in New York, but I saw the face of your problem on TV. Ain't she a pretty girl… It's all over the news."

"I called Sarah."

"I know that too, I just got off the phone with her. I'll be home early, tonight at the latest."

"Get here as soon as you can because you don't know the whole thing. I found a note this morning in my mailbox. Well, it's more like a card, actually. I know it's from her!"

I'm out of breath, and Archie realizes it.

"That's annoying… What does the card say? Is it threatening?"

"Yes, you've got to tell me what you think about it."

"You're scaring me… I'll be there soon."

And he hangs up.

I've never been a man of secrets – my life is actually as unmysterious as it can get. Like many in this city, I work a lot, have an interesting job, take few vacations, and earn good money. What is ruining my life started early last fall, as I was parked along the sidewalk at the bottom of the big hill at Brunswick. Engine purring, parking brake on, I wanted to call the newspaper I worked for but my phone had run out of battery in the early afternoon so I had to plug it into the USB socket on the dashboard. Fumbling in the glove box for the charger, I saw a kid riding his skateboard at full speed towards me. The noise was deafening when he hit my front fender full force.

Upon impact, the colorful, varnished board and the child in shorts soared across the hood before crashing on the asphalt.

I rushed to his side. The street was empty and the child not moving. He was breathing so I didn't move him, but he was lying in the middle of a crossroads and I was scared that he would get run over. A half second and an urgent need to protect him later, I got into my car and moved it in front of him. Soon, other cars arrived and I signaled them to stop, to call for help. A woman parked next to me and got out, a big leather briefcase in hand.

"I'm a doctor, make room for the ambulance!"

Getting back into my car, I parked further away. As I got out, I looked at where the kid had hit me. Not a single impact on the car, the skateboard having only hit the front tire where a white mark was visible. The kid had flown over the hood before collapsing on the road. An NYPD Ford with a blaring siren snuck up on the crowd of onlookers, staring at the child's lifeless body. The Ford blocked the road and a cop got out to clear the intersection before the paramedics arrived. The overturned skateboard was on the sidewalk, only a few meters from the kid, suggesting that he hadn't been able to slow down in time, losing control and falling hard. This wasn't the first time a kid had crashed at the bottom of the hill. But until then, kids had always gotten away with bruises and bumps.

The cops started to try to figure out what had happened. I almost went to them and explained but stopped at the last moment, thinking that they wouldn't believe me. I felt strangely responsible, almost guilty for having been at the wrong place at the wrong time. This feeling made me uncomfortable, no matter how much I told myself that I wasn't to blame and that I was parked correctly. I couldn't bring myself to face my involuntary involvement.

To this day, I still don't know if I was to blame or not. On second thought, if I wasn't, I didn't have anyone to testify so it would be difficult to prove that I was parked in a regular spot, at a full stop. On the other hand, I'd just had a long lunch and I wasn't sure if I would have tested negative for alcohol. The slightest violation of the legal limit would allow a pugnacious prosecutor to disregard my testimony. If the child died, I'd end up in prison.

I had in mind the appalling story of a sixty-four years old man who had just been released from a Missouri penitentiary by an inmate aid organization after thirty-four years of captivity when he was perfectly innocent. Seeing him on TV had deeply shocked me, making me question our justice system's impartiality and infallibility. I still waited for the ambulance to drive the child away, an ambulance I followed to find out the name of the hospital that would treat him. Ever since that fateful day, I'd been checking on him through Archie who knew a nurse there. The accident happened in the blink of an eye and the street was completely empty. No one had seen me and no witness had come forward to the police.

How could Mario's mother have linked the accident to me?
Who told her?
Who saw me?
So many unanswered questions.

The phone in the living room was ringing again. I try to resist the urge to answer with the help of Mariza's voice. It's crazy, but I know that this madwoman will call me. I wait with one hand on the phone, but it's too late when I make up my mind: the call has gone to my answering machine. I hear myself ramble the usual greeting message. Silence stretches before a woman's voice fills the room, freezing my blood. The voice is young, soft, measured, and strangely neutral. She sings a lullaby, the tune familiar. The words are incomprehensible, a kind of Spanish patois like the one I heard during my trips to Latin America. I understand instinctively that this is the voice I'm dreading to hear. It's Liliana Morales. Suddenly, I'm drenched in sweat and full-blown panicking. Before I can think twice about it, I pick up the phone and cut her off.

"Mrs. Morales, please wait! I can explain!"

But it's too late and the line is silent. I freeze, the phone to my ear, my spine cold, and my heart beating too fast.

"Fuck you, Liliana Morales!" I scream.

Raging, I insult her for a long time to exorcise the horror that knotted my guts. With Liliana out for my blood, I think swearing will be as necessary for my survival as the sweet words I used to whisper to my girlfriend when I had one.

The doorbell rings three times in a row, making me jump. Archie always rings three times.

I'll finally get the answer to my question.

Did he tell anyone else but Sarah?

8

I unlock the door but stop before opening it, freezing. The wide-angle camera on the landing is showing emptiness. The only way to be out of frame is to duck low against the door. I don't have time to lock the door again, hearing a metal sound in the lock and feeling the door open.

In the hallway, on his knees with a thin metal blade in his hand, Archie looks at me with a tense but reassuring smile.

"You did exactly the one thing you shouldn't have."

"God, you scared the hell out of me!"

"Good, because if it had been the crazy one, you wouldn't be walking this Earth anymore!"

"Not everyone knows how to pick locks."

"It's a lot easier than you think."

With a worried crease on his forehead, Archie puts the blade back in the khaki bag at his feet, gathers the straps, and picks it up with unusual precaution.

"Come in!"

He wipes his feet for a long time like he always does before passing the threshold, his ever so impressive build counteracting his angelic face. He must have had to bend over backward to hide from the camera. I'm so glad that he's here that I'm seconds away from hugging him. Everyone needs moral support and a solid physical presence in complicated life moments. What I have here is a friend but also, even if it's from another life, an experienced soldier, skilled in armed combat.

"Archie, I've got to tell you about –"

"I know, the entire country's talking about it. The FBI's on it too."

"What you don't know yet is what she sent me!"

"Show me."

I hand him Liliana's message, my fingers shaking with anger – or maybe fear. As he reads it, Archie's forehead wrinkles. He goes over it several times, walking with the card in his hands before sitting down on the sofa. I play him my answering machine, and the killer's voice fills the space again. It's hard for me not to stop the recording of this warmonger singing a lullaby.

"It's clear now, she wants me dead. I'm not making it up!"

He looks at me with a sigh, points with his chin to the Beretta in its holster still on the coffee table, and picks up the bag he has put on the floor.

"The gun's good. But heavy artillery is always better, so I brought what you needed."

He bends down, opens the long bag, and pulls out a Remington 870 rifle. I recognize the Marine Corps weapon that has been used by the Army since the 1950s, familiar to every gun-owning American.

"Twelve gauges, you have seven shots."

"What do you want me to do with that?"

"Protect yourself. This woman isn't only crazy, she would be insane enough to come here, at home, to get you."

"Easy soldier, we're not there yet!"

"We don't know that. And when we don't know…"

I nod. He's not wrong, so I take the gun. He hands me a box of magazines that I refuse with a small wave.

"Maybe the loading part can wait."

"No, it can't. Do you even know how to use it?"

"Well, when I was in the army I've been around, spent many years in war zones."

"That's funny, care to remind me where you were stationed?"

"In the staff offices."

"How many times did you shoot as a correspondent?"

"I never did."

68

Archie starts laughing. "Look, it's not rocket science."

He takes the rifle from my hands and silently loads it. The operation doesn't last more than three seconds but I watch him attentively. His movements are quick and precise – this guy is elegant even loading a deadly rifle. I feel like I'm witnessing the start of a manhunt. Archie puts the safety on and puts the rifle on the coffee table. He looks at me, worried but pleased with his performance. I ask him the question that has been itching my throat since he arrived.

"Archie, please swear you never told anyone about this."

He's not surprised. "I wondered the same thing. The answer is no one except Sarah. Rest assured, she's worse than me! She wouldn't have shared your secret."

"I don't understand then. How did she find out about me?"

"Well, I know."

"What do you mean, you know?"

"It was Pepita Diaz, the owner of the fast-food restaurant who spotted you when you parked. There aren't many coupés like yours that park in Brunswick, especially driven by a white man."

"How do you know that?"

"I didn't tell you because I didn't want to freak you out, but the week after the kid's accident, I went to hang out there and had a few beers at the Diaz's joint. From the bar, you have a panoramic view of the intersection. The owner liked that I was an ex-military mess. These people always need experts."

"You, ex-military mess?"

"I had to put on a show to get her to tell me more about what was still the talk of the coffee shop. On the day of the accident, the restaurant was closed, so there weren't many people around, except for her. She was sitting at a table, balancing her checkbook. She heard the crash of the skateboard against your car and rushed to see what was going on."

"So if she knows what happened, she also knows that I had nothing to do with it!"

"She saw you getting out of the car but she didn't see the accident. She's convinced that you hit Mario."

"Then why didn't she tell that to the cops?"

"It's not really the style of the house. Pepita's not a model citizen. But she did write down your license plate so she could find you later."

"I don't get it."

"Spencer, you know Brunswick is run by Latinos, right? The Perls' gang."

"Yeah, so what?"

"The owner of the bar is having an affair with one of the mob's bosses. She's also, and this is where you'll understand, Liliana's cousin. She's the one who was in charge of the kid while his mother was working."

"Dear God, what a mess...!"

"It gets worse. The back room of the restaurant is their head-quarters. Call it family solidarity or whatnot, but they promised the kid's mother to find you. Which, apparently, they did."

"It's a fucking nightmare! What am I supposed to do? How am I supposed to get out of this shithole alive with a gang tracking me down and maybe a price on my head?"

Archie, forehead still creased, stays silent for a beat before resuming confidently.

"If you want my take on it, the Perls' gang won't interfere in Liliana's business – it's too messy. Look, I can take care of Liliana. Believe me, if war is what she wants, war is what she's going to get. And open warfare isn't too good for her fugitive run either –"

Archie is a veteran, a real professional – he's seen it all on the battlefield. A madwoman, no matter how deranged, won't be enough to impress him. He's been trained to get out of the worst situations. He should be able to help me get out of mine.

I stop biting my nails and interrupt him. "We have to find a solution..."

"We will."

"I hope you're right. This mess is twisting my guts, it's making me sick. I'm way too old for this bullshit. We're not twenty anymore!"

"Precisely. We're cautious and experienced."

"This woman isn't even thirty..."

"You know how the young recruits, the kids in uniform are. I've seen them get shot like balloons at the fair!"

"Maybe, but she's still dangerous. Escaping from a hospital's penitentiary is insane..."

"She has to have a weakness."

"The only one I know is her son, Mario. The kid's in a coma, she'll try to see him at some point."

Archie is sporting a skeptical pout. He waits before throwing in the silence of the apartment a "I'm not sure, Spencer."

"You're not sure? She escaped for that sole purpose."

"I don't think so. I mean, that's not her main goal."

"What do you mean?"

"Think about it. Her son is in a coma that he won't come out of. She knows it and, in my opinion, he's already dead to her."

"Why did she escape then? Revenge?"

"That's what I'm afraid of."

I physically feel the blow. The already heavy silence turns into a lead canopy. I get up, go to the kitchen and come back shaking my head.

"Archie, how can we get in touch with her? To talk to her?"

"I don't know. I don't think it's possible, but we'll look into it."

"Because, for God's sake, all we have to do is explain the situation. It's not my fault that this kid hit my car – it was at a full stop. Goddamnit, the only time I do pull over to make a phone call!"

"She wouldn't believe you anyway. Maybe the kid could convince her, but not in the state he's in."

I feel like the sky is getting darker. I need air. I need to breathe.

"Excuse me, Archie, I didn't even offer you a drink."

"I was wondering when you would."

His reassuring smile accompanies me to the kitchen where I pull out two beers. Archie takes his lighter out of his pocket, uses it as a prop, and uncaps his while I hand him mine. When he gives it back to me, I must be wincing.

"Don't worry, Spencer, we'll get through this."

"I feel like I'm stuck in a fishbowl, Archie."

"When you're stuck, what you do is think first and then react, not the other way around."

"What are you suggesting?"

"First, hide. Then, if necessary, shoot."

"That's some hostile mercenary logic."

"Please, I've never been a mercenary."

"Sorry, I'm on edge."

"I may not be twenty anymore, but I'm still a good professional. I train regularly with over-trained kids that are fifteen years younger than me and still have the upper hand. This featherweight has no idea what I can put her through."

"Archie, that's what bothers me… This woman, that you don't take seriously enough, is completely out of her depth. She's unpredictable, and could be a much bigger problem than you think."

"Possibly. But as good as she is, I don't give her a month before she waves the white flag and runs back to where she came from. Don't forget that she has every cop in the country on her tail."

"A month is both short and very long."

"Don't worry about it, just keep the rifle close to you. Do you have other weapons?"

72

"Apart from this brand-new Beretta? Nothing."

"It's a good weapon. Have it with you at all times."

"Archie, I forgot to tell you. She was in the military and was trained by one of the best units in the Cuban army. Then again, it's not West Point."

Archie almost chokes and puts the bottle down. "Are you sure about this? Because that's a total game-changer. Fuck!"

"I read it on an FBI file."

"How reliable is your source?"

I shrug, raise my eyebrows and take a long sip. "Very. He's an ace intelligence officer. He can be trusted."

Archie has a worried look on his face that I've never seen before. He stares at me.

"With this info in mind, I doubt that we'll catch her quickly. I understand better why, if not how, she escaped from the hospital."

"How is no longer a mystery, I'll have you read the officer's notes. It's worthy of a film noir. She's batshit crazy!"

"Let me fix it once and for all!"

"What do you mean? What do you have in mind? You're scaring me."

"Nothing's set in stone. Let's start with you: you're coming to my place, there's no way you're staying here."

"No, Archie. I'll be waiting for her right here, on a terrain that I know well. If she comes, I'll neutralize her and explain everything."

Archie shrugs, his eyes closed halfway, his face frozen, his body looking small. He looks like a wild animal – I've never seen him like this. For the first time, I catch a glimpse of the fighter under his thick shell.

He resumes with a fatalistic smile. "If she comes inside and if what you told me is true, Spencer, you don't have a fighting chance."

"Don't be so dramatic!"

"She's Cuban, Spencer, and if she's been trained by one of Castro's elite units, she's learned a lot of things they don't teach in girls' school... How to shoot, how to fight, and how to kill, but also how to blend in whether the environment is hostile or not!"

"I've read all that. What do you want me to say, Archie? The fact remains that she's also a woman and she's not invincible. I'm not going to take night classes in urban guerrilla fighting either!"

He shrugs violently. "We're not in the same league anymore! Give me your spare keys. Call me as soon as something's not right. In the meantime, I'll see what I can do."

It's not Archie but the First Lieutenant who gets up from the couch. Bolting upright, he chugs back his beer, puts it on the coffee table, picks up the Beretta, loads it, and puts it back in its holster. A quick hug later, he's walking out the door. "Watch out. Don't open the door – I'll call you beforehand next time I drop by."

9

With Archie gone, silence weighs on me. I hear a police siren speed up the avenue traffic. The cops are all on edge, their shotguns loaded and ready to burst from their holsters, all within reach in every car, while none of them ever gets home on time.

It's their biggest hunt of the season.

The mayor has asked for and received reinforcements from the inner suburbs to secure Manhattan. A new murder would be a delicate blow to a municipality that has zero-tolerance for crimes. Voices are beginning to be heard, condemning the carelessness of the police force, unable to put their hands on a young, mentally ill woman.

I pour myself a drink. I need to have familiar gestures, habits that reassure me. I need to regain my composure. It's not like I was in the middle of a street fight, wearing a heavy helmet and a bulletproof vest, between two enemy militias who were doing their best to exterminate the other.

The observation is simple.

How will Liliana Morales get into the building?

The lobby is secured with a concierge and cameras. But Archie told me that this wouldn't stop her.

What the hell are the cops doing?

The sicko can't be that hard to locate. I look at Archie's rifle on the coffee table, right next to the gun, deciding that I'll put it on my belt holster later. God, I'm not ready yet. I already feel over-armed. With this arsenal, I can hold out until the cavalry arrives. As ravaged and combative as she might be, this woman isn't bulletproof.

Beware, Morales, I'll put a hole in you if you dare come into my house!

What a nice declaration of intent. I'm playing the warrior here and it's making me feel better. This woman is a soldier, some kind of female ninja, while I hardly know how to handle a gun. The last time I fired was in the army, twenty-five years ago.

Over the phone, Blatters, my shrink, warned me that she was smarter than she looked and that she shouldn't be underestimated. Her pathology didn't lead to any intellectual weakness, quite the opposite. I asked him to clarify a few things for me.

"John, she's a sociopath, all right. Then why is the media talking about a psychopath?"

I can still hear him explain. "It's a tale as old as time, Spencer. We know psychopaths and it sounds better… A crime paired with psychopathy is a rating spiker!"

"She's not far from psychopathy either, killing as she pleases!"

"Not very far, yes. The pathologies are similar on many points."

"It's crazy that we aren't able to spot her! It doesn't take a Ph.D. to see that she has a problem."

"Apart from an intense and staring, unblinking look, her neurosis isn't visible. It doesn't show, she looks like me and you."

"Do you find a staring gaze and eyes that never blink normal, doctor?"

"It takes a trained eye to diagnose mental abnormality. This is where sociopathy is dangerous, because it hides and remains mostly invisible. The patients suffer but don't feel sick."

"In other words, she can be at the local drugstore picking out her lunchtime shopping without anyone noticing her?"

"That's right. Or at the hairdresser's, getting her hair dyed."

The shrink had explained the disease in detail. I understood that Liliana, despite appearances, was the first victim. She suffered much more than we imagined. Already unstable and anxious, it doesn't take much for a sociopath to trigger an overreaction or an aggressive impulse. All it takes is frustration, annoyance, or a latent and prolonged bad influence from family and entourage.

And as far as family was concerned, she'd gotten the short end of the stick. Poverty, violence, the death of her mother, and her father's sexual aggressions had turned the sweet young girl into a merciless harpy that didn't know limits. The doctors dated the onset of the disease to just after her first rape. As proof, the emotional shock that she hadn't felt, or almost hadn't felt, when she should have been terribly traumatized. Since this fateful night, Liliana had had this evil grow in her, a water lily growing inside her brain. She suffered more from it than anyone else and wasn't able to soften the pain or fight it. In the span of a few years, she became more insensitive to the suffering of her peers.

Mario was the only exception.

Liliana no longer understood the world that she lived in and no longer had any respect for the laws that governed it. She went her own way without caring about the damage she left behind. When an obstacle occurred, she'd knock it down without even thinking about going around it. This manipulative, destructive behavior never led to guilt but to a kind of indifference and a feeling of total irresponsibility.

According to Blatters, this illness was incurable in the long run but could be treated – there were therapies to soften the aggressive outbursts. That hadn't been the case for Liliana.

In both hospitals and women's prison facilities, the prisoners don't have any emotional life and little to no visits from their loved ones. The deprivation of Liliana's son and the 23-hours daily confinement slowed down the effect of the medication protocols ordered by the doctors.

The shock of Mario's accident added to the administration's very firm and stupid refusal to allow her to run to her son's bedside, even if only for a few minutes, threw her back into the depths of her illness and destroyed a therapy that had lasted several months. From that day on, she had only one thought racing in her mind. One goal to help her survive her terrible anxiety and her nightmares.

Destroying the one person she held responsible for Mario's accident.

I pour myself an umpteenth coffee. A vengeful, murdering madwoman on the loose, whose only obsession is killing me? I couldn't believe it. I suddenly feel my stomach twist and my mouth dry up.

The lack of understanding that I have of this woman is eating me alive. She's devoured by an illness that no one can remove from her brain and it's making me crazy too. I'm wandering aimlessly in my big yuppie Manhattan living room, and so is my timid intellectual mind, unable to come up with a solution.

I've opened the French doors to the terrace.

My apartment, on the seventeenth floor, is a natural fortress – at least that's what I'm trying to tell myself. Outside, the shrubs in their pots are suffering from the unusual autumn dryness; it's been at least two months since it last rained. They dangerously need to be watered. I'll reconnect the automatic sprinkler for the night. Right next to me is the watering can, waiting to be filled. I make up my mind, thinking that it'll make me think of something else. As I pour the water, I try not to think of an armed Liliana, ambushed in the building across the street.

Earlier, Archie seemed worried despite his assurance and his concern stresses me down to the bone. The phone rings, I rush. It's John Blatters. He tells me that Liliana Morales was seen the day before in Washington Square, right by my building.

But was it really her? There's no proof. She disappeared before the police could arrest her.

"Did you notice anything unusual, Spencer?"

"I haven't left my house since this morning."

"Well, don't."

"Are you sure of this info? Or are these rumors? People often make up things in these kinds of stressful situations."

"You're right. People are seeing her everywhere and the police is overwhelmed with incoming calls. But this one seems plausible according to the agent I had on the phone earlier."

I don't reply. My stomach is getting more knotted. What is there to say?

"All right, Spencer, I'll come by as soon as I can. Just be careful when your doorbell rings, and don't open unless you're sure!"

This is the second time I've been told not to open to just anyone. As for Liliana's presence near my place, I remain skeptical. I don't see her walking in the square in broad daylight, French fries in hand, while the cops are swarming the area.

I don't believe it. I don't want to believe it. She can't have quietly reached the hall to the mailboxes to slip the envelope too, it has to have been an accomplice. To prove to myself that I'm right not to panic, I put Archie's gun away in the front closet. My door is armored, ten points of anchorage, the lock locked: it would take TNT to break in.

It's late and I'm not sleepy. I take two pills and a big swing of scotch before going to bed. Tomorrow's a brand new day. Not wasting time counting sheep, I fall asleep right away.

Good thing I doubled the intake.

After her escape from the hospital, Liliana had sought shelter in Brooklyn with Pepita. Cousin Diaz and her mobster husband had welcomed her without enthusiasm, aware of the risk, but they had caved and gave her a place to stay until the cops looked for her somewhere that wasn't New York anymore.

Family was family.

Liliana's first trip to Manhattan to slip her souvenir card into Spencer Hogg's mailbox had almost gone wrong. On the way back, a subway agent had recognized her and called the cops – she'd been close to being caught. Her family hadn't liked it and told her bluntly. The culprit had to go to Max, a former dentist convicted for insurance fraud now turned tattoo artist and hairstylist. He was a miracle worker, specializing in new looks for those who needed to change theirs. He was a strange but brilliant guy with fantastic dexterity when it came to transforming a face. Liliana had resisted, she didn't see the need for such a change, but the cousins had insisted. Pepita Diaz's mind was set: it was either that or the door, meaning insecurity for her son and the dangers of the streets for her.

Max, sporting rolled white coat sleeves over the tattoos on his forearms, received more thugs than honest people, which is why he didn't want to know anything about his clients or the reasons why they came to change their identities. He worked on the first floor of a Bronx building, in his tattoo shop. The backroom looked like a dental clinic because of the medical chair sitting in the middle of the room. He began by taking a few pictures of Liliana, uploaded them on his laptop, and worked on Photoshoping her face. He was quick and silent, focused on the task at hand.

She waited patiently. When he was done, he printed a picture, asked her to take off her blouse and bra to put on a medical scrub, had her sit on the chair that he tilted horizontally, and began the metamorphosis.

Five hours later, Liliana looked older. He bleached her hair a platinum blonde color, straightened it, added extensions, and cut bangs that hid half her face. Liliana, who never wore any make-up, now knew how to put on blush and lipstick to look older, classier, and more American. She was taller too thanks to the ten-centimeters heels on her feet. Max handed her a push-up bra to increase her chest size, put emerald green cosmetic contact lenses in her eyes, and finished the job by extracting her first two upper molars to hollow out her cheeks and enhance her cheekbones. The anesthetic part hadn't gone too well since she feared it was a Pepita trick to get rid of her. Max had to stab the needle in his own arm fat to show her that it was indeed anesthetic and not poison. To check that the muscle was asleep, she stuck a needle in his biceps and he hadn't winced.

She'd left the makeover exhausted, stressed but transformed. The shop showcases reflected a Liliana she didn't know – even her son Mario wouldn't have recognized her. The cops who were patrolling were looking for a young Cuban woman, a brunette with short hair, neurotic with hooded sweatshirts, Levi's jeans and sneakers, not a tall and slim forty-year-old woman with pumps, long blond hair, beautiful green eyes, prominent cheekbones, more sophisticated than dangerous Fidel Castro muse. Liliana had successfully completed her cousin's ultimatum: her metamorphosis was insanely good. She looked like a sexy, middle-class forty-years-old, and she looked better with light, straightened hair.

Pepita and her drug lord husband had quickly managed to get her a fake ID to match her new looks and had put her behind the bar during the evenings. They weren't about to feed and protect her for free while she hung around all day doing nothing. Not to mention, the neighborhood was filled with spotters on the lookout working for the gang… No cop could hang out in their streets without being seen. Liliana, blood or not, had to keep her nose out of everyone's business if she didn't want to end up back on the sidewalk or in a whorehouse. The Diaz couple didn't want her back with the cops: she knew too much about their juicy dope traffic. The people hanging at the fast-food were miles away from thinking that the beautiful blonde waitress was one of Manhattan's most wanted criminals and that she could just as easily pour them a scotch or stab them straight into the heart.

As the weeks flew by, the stress lessened. Liliana wasn't a drama queen, letting the customers slap her butt without a reaction. She had only one obsession, and one obsession only: to see her son again and to kill the one man responsible for his accident. At Saint George's hospital, the doctors were trying new protocols, but Mario was still in a coma.

Liliana, who was feeling relatively safe since her change of looks, took a time-out to think about a plan. The only problem was that she had to go out to scout out possible scenarios and risked having her ID checked by the cops. Hatred had a firm grip around her heart since she knew who had caused the accident, thanks to her cousin that helped her track down Spencer Hogg. The Chevrolet coupé had caught the eye of a few people; finding the name of its owner had been easier than expected.

Pepita got the help of a dashing 50 years old Cuban who worked at the Manhattan courthouse and had access to police files. He regularly spent his evenings at the Diaz's restaurant and had a weakness for pretty brunettes. He jumped on the occasion and came back one evening with a smile on his face and a file in his hand. Pepita thanked him just the way he hoped and all's well would have ended well if the story had stopped there. Except that the man, exhilarated by reward, made the mistake of wanting to know the reason behind his file delivery, and wanting more rewards. Faced with a hard no, he threatened to tell Spencer Hogg about the Diaz's sudden interest in him; in return, Spencer Hogg would have undoubtedly wanted to know why his license plate was on a desk at a bad fast-food restaurant in the Bronx. Pepita wasn't happy about the blackmail and wasn't the kind of woman to let others deal with her problems. This small hiccup was dealt with one moonless night, and his head was found the next morning in a gutter.

The autopsy revealed enough crack in his blood to kill an elephant. The same kind of drug, with the same chemical composition, as the rocks sold in the neighborhood's streets by the Perls dealers led by Pepita's husband. The crack sold by the gang had more than 80% of pure cocaine and, if you weren't careful, you could OD in less than five minutes.

The court where the Cuban worked covered up the case. Justice didn't like to be judged or to judge its peers.

10

Ever since Liliana had been bartending at night instead of Pepita, she'd been unrecognizable but her beauty still turned heads. Her beautiful green eyes that never blinked often shone, especially when she thought of Spencer Hogg. Her gaze only softened when she thought of her son, Mario. When her shift was over, she'd sleep for a few hours and then go prowling in the Manhattan streets until morning to find out Spencer's daily habits. However, the cops at the Fifth Avenue police station, who thought at first that she was a prostitute, soon noticed her existence. They realized too late that she was *the* Liliana Morales. The criminal. She had to run away quickly, but not without noticing the old lady begging in a remote corner of the building across Spencer's.

That's when a plan began to form in her mad head. She needed an observation post, and the beggar woman's was perfect.

The Brunswick restaurant was closed on Sundays – it was a day off for Liliana and the staff. She waited for nighttime and rode the subway with a hammer hidden in her bag. There was always a crowd in the evening on the weekends, meaning that she was able to get close without raising the attention of the patrolling cops or of the old woman who was holding out her hand in hopes of getting coins with a complaint on her lips. Instead of coins, she got a hammer blow straight on her wrist, breaking it. She cried from the pain and fainted but Liliana made her come to with a kick in the ribs. Bending over her, the iron of the hammer crushing the woman's mouth, she whispered in a soft voice: "Get out of here and never come back or I'll end you. Understood, Grandma?"

The old lady, who was shaking from pain and fear, had to flee, leaving behind the small belongings she had.

On her way back to Brunswick, Liliana called Max from a payphone to ask him if he could turn her into an old woman, preferably a beggar. He hesitated for a minute but when she tripled the price that she first paid, he told her to meet him at the shop.

As a precaution, she went through a back door that opened into a narrow dead-end street. For a few days, he'd been noticing strange comings and goings and he'd smelled an unmistakable smell of the feds. But so many people came in and out of his hairdresser's, tattooist's and facialist's shop that he tuned down the feeling. He'd just have to be more careful than usual.

Through the dead-end, Liliana easily reached the back of the shop, right under the nose of the cops stationed on the second floor of the building facing Max's shop. She was foaming with barely contained rage.

"It stinks around here, I can feel the cops. You gave me up, you son of a bitch?"

"Hell no! You're making things up. Tell me what you want and what you want it for."

"I want forty more years. You don't have to know why, just get moving. Cops make me nervous…"

Max had a hard time calming her down. He sat her in the dental chair and quickly drew a bunch of extra wrinkles on her face before gluing them on. Once he was done, he gathered her hair in a net and put a grey wig on. He wrapped the whole thing in an old, dark scarf that was large enough to hide most of her face, gave her round glasses with thick PVC frames, and draped her body in a huge grey shawl before handing her a bag in tatters and a cheap cane.

"There, put on these old shoes and you'll be done, no need for more."

"You don't put more makeup on?"

84

"You told me you wanted to look okay from a distance. Now, if you want to look realistic up close and without a scarf, that's a whole other story!"

Liliana checked her reflection in the mirror that lined the entire back of the store and was impressed. This guy was a genius; he would have made a fortune in Hollywood relooking stars with identity crises. Max was satisfied with his work too, it was never easy to add or remove twenty years to a face without butchering it. But he knew how to do it better than anyone else.

"Nice work, Max. You're definitely worth the hype!"

He didn't reply. He wanted her to pay and to leave now that the work was done. His instincts were telling him that she was dangerous and that being near her was like sitting on a barrel of TNT. Liliana had been eager at the beginning but was now dragging things out.

"Well, I'll pay what I owe you. But before I go, could you get me a gun? An automatic one?"

The tattoo artist wasn't expecting that and tried to skive off. The woman stepped right into his face, almost touching him. She was as tall as him.

"Max, do you know who I am?"

He lowered his eyes, embarrassed by the question and her proximity. He could smell her perfume, a mix of musk and sweat.

"No. The Perls gang sent you here, that's all I know. I never ask my customers who they are and I don't want to know. It's a rule that I never stray away from!"

It was hard for him to articulate. She smiled before answering. This man, no matter how gifted, wasn't about to fuck her over. The inner Liliana Morales soldier learned during her training in Cuba how to tell apart people who were lying and people who weren't. Max was undoubtedly lying. She pushed and stepped even closer, violating his privacy on purpose like she'd been taught.

"I'm sure you have a clue, don't you?"

85

Preach the false to get the truth, also known as intel 101. Like she'd planned, he stepped back abruptly and forced a laugh, hoping to soothe the tension.

With an insecure voice, he added in one go. "No, I swear, I don't. Clues kill too many people around here. Please stop moving or you'll peel off the wrinkles I glued –"

She cut him off. "All right, I'll take your word for it. But you'll still be doing me a favor."

"Anything."

"I need a weapon. A Colt, or another small gun."

Max jumped. Weapons weren't his thing, and their traffic even less.

He tried to play it cool. "I've got a lot of things here, but not that, not yet. Sorry…"

Liliana looked annoyed and went back to sit in the dental chair. "I can pay," she uncrossed her legs, "or more."

Max felt an adrenaline rush and he wasn't sure if it was fear or lust. There was this insane but beautiful woman with her thighs open, willing to give him money and pleasure. It was surreal. Liliana was ready to be used and even had a sudden desire to be. It had been a long time since she'd had an orgasm. She's always had a thing for big tattooed guys with long curly hair and a big beard. The tattoo artist was probably good in bed, he'd drill the way she liked. It was hard for Max to pass the opportunity, but he knew who this pretty woman was and both her recent and past crimes. Pepita had given him vague information, asking him not to upset her.

He extricated himself from the situation with a promise that didn't mean anything. "Leave me your number and I'll call when I have something in store."

Liliana closed her legs, her face pale despite the make-up.

"You don't call me, I call you."

Her tone was icy cold. Getting up from the seat, she looked at her reflection again and bent over to imitate an old woman.

It was perfect. Max was relieved: she was paying him and leaving; he'd just have to find a good excuse when she'll eventually call. He was used to dealing with thugs and his cunning was the same as his clients'. Relieved, he turned around and began to put away his make-up brushes to show that the service was done and that it was time for her to get going.

Max didn't pay attention when she picked her bag from the floor, but something made him jump a little. Whatever kind of alarm blasted in his mind, it was too late. Maybe it was the quick shadow cast by the surgical table on the opposite wall or maybe it was the abnormal and too close crumpling of a piece of clothing carrying a violent movement. Whatever it was, he barely felt the air moved by the hammer before it sank a good half into his skull.

This one won't talk anymore, Liliana thought as she stepped back to avoid being splashed by the blood spurting from his head.

Her heart didn't skip a beat as she spat repeatedly on an agonizing Max, lying on the cold tile of the back room. It was actually the opposite. This murder made her feel better. She hadn't come for that, but she was glad to have thought of it. If, as she believed, the cops were watching him, it meant that they had a tail. There was no way she was going to let a guy live, no matter how useful he was, knowing who she was and where she could be found. Max had both of these pieces of information. The link to Brunswick's cousin Diaz was too obvious and he was too smart to ignore it.

Had they arrested him, the feds would have eaten him alive. Liliana knew that he would have spilled every bit of info he had without looking back twice if it meant saving himself. She was right to do what she'd done. Now, all was left to do was find the weapon she needed to kill Spencer Hogg. Max was American, wasn't he? He had to have one hidden somewhere. She looked in every nook of the shop without any luck. The guy didn't have a gun – he must have been the exception to the rule. When in the army, she'd been taught that for every hundred Americans, there were a hundred and one guns. Liliana had met the one person who didn't fit the concept, probably a peace-and-love kind of man. There had indeed been something hippie in Max.

In a fit of rage, she pulled the hammer out of his skull, wiped it on his blue scrub, and insulted him, his mother, and all his ancestors. She turned the shop's door sign to "closed", went out through the dead-end again, but instead of running away, she challengingly went around the block and up the street from where she could feel the ambushing cops. Lingering in front of the shop for a moment, she stared at the building across the street through the glass. It didn't take her long before spotting the camera behind one of the windows on the second floor. She frowned and pursed her lips, barely holding back from stomping up to the feds' hideout and surprising them. If only she had a gun. Instead, she grumbled, spat on the sidewalk, and walked away with the slow pace of an old lady.

The next day, dressed in the clothes of a beggar, skillfully aged, glasses perched on her nose and wrap on her head, Liliana stood in the darkest corner of the building that faced Spencer's. The passers-by were used to this shapeless figure, so no one paid attention to the change. During the following weeks, she was able to monitor who came into the building and who left.

Pepita, who was impatient to have her out of the restaurant, had given her a picture of Spencer Hogg that she'd found online. Liliana just had to look up to see Spencer come and go, almost always with Archie. The two friends went out two or three times a week for beers at Kate's. She had followed them and it was only Archie's presence and build that had kept her from jumping on them.

Fall had taken residency in Manhattan's streets. Insensitive to cold, expressionless face, fixed stare that sociopaths tend to have, Liliana was still hiding in plain sight, weaving her web right under the noses of all those who were looking for her. Max's murder had caused a stir in the Bronx Cuban community. It wasn't difficult for the cops to put two and two together and identify the culprit, especially when his hair and spit were on the victim's face. Liliana Morales' DNA had spoken but the police force was careful and kept the info private.

Even the Diaz couple didn't have the slightest idea of who to blame.

11

A month had passed since the escape, and still not a single sighting of Liliana. I'm convinced that she went back to Cuba. This permanent fear eats me up inside and I'm scared, I'll soon be afraid of my shadow. I'd prefer calls on my phone and rings on my doorbell to this silent treatment. The gun is still on the table with its magazine.

The phone rings and startles me. An overexcited John Blatters is yelling in my ear, the ground shaking beneath my feet.

"Spencer!"

"John?"

"Thank God you're here! Did you hear?"

"Hear what?"

My stomach's all twisted. Ever since Liliana Morales' escape, ever since the note I found in my mailbox, I've been preparing myself for the worst, and I know that my shrink has a front row-seat to the bad news.

"About Mario! He woke up last night."

I couldn't believe it. "He what?"

"He came to! Mario is out of the woods now. He was already showing signs that he'd wake up last week but I didn't want to say anything in case he didn't."

"Are you sure?"

"He spoke. He's waking up slowly but he's getting there."

"What do you mean, he spoke?"

"Just a few words. He asked to see his mother – it shows that his memory isn't impaired."

"That's crazy… I don't know what to say."

"Me neither when I first heard about it this morning!"

"Who told you?"

"The doctor who has been treating him since he was admitted, Professor Judson. He's an expert, you can trust him. If he says the boy will be fine, he will!"

"I hope so... This is too much. I need some time to think this through."

"We don't have much time, Spencer. Liliana Morales is still dangerous and on the loose. Judson wants to know more about Mario's medical file and he needs info that only she can give him. He's convinced that she would be very useful for his recovery. She's his mother, whether we like it or not."

I don't see how her being on the run could contribute to Mario's healing. I'm sure it's purely wishing upon a star at this point but I have to ask him. "John, please try to find out if Mario remembers the accident. It's crucial."

"I will. I have to meet Judson at Saint George's, we'll talk later."

"Call me when you come back from the hospital!" I implore, but John has already hung up.

The news of the kid waking up has shaken me with a bliss that I can't give into yet, even if this happiness snatched from fate must be consumed immediately. Mario is unplugged and I'm the one who's having trouble breathing. The kid is back to life, cheating the odds like a lottery winner. He'll be able to step out of his diapers, live, smile, and explain everything to his mother. The nightmare is about to end. I turn on the news channel, convinced that they'll talk about it for hours on end. Liliana Morales will learn about it very soon too. In the meantime, I jog down to the supermarket for some grocery shopping. I'm ravenous, it's like the news has unknotted my stomach. It's been twisted for a whole month; I've lost five kilos and I didn't have much fat to begin with. I'm not afraid of Liliana anymore. If I met her, I'd say: *I had nothing to do with it, ask your son!*

Liliana was psychopathic or sociopathic, sure, but also intelligent and, therefore, not that crazy. She can think and only resents people who hurt her or prevent her from doing what she wants. This woman, according to Blatters, is driven by violent, irrepressible impulses, but there's always a reason behind her behavior. I rescued her son, stopped the cars from running him over, called 911, did what had to be done to keep him safe. *For God's sake, I didn't run away like a criminal!*

I'd like to believe that I'm the grand savior but I'm making it up, choosing to forget that the car that Mario hit was mine and not someone else's. A nice speech won't be enough – she'll need proof. She'll need to see her son, she'll need to talk to him or he'll need to tell her. How can we get the cops to let her through to him? I'll ask Blatters to ask Mario to record his answer and to give it to the media. The nightmare will be over soon.

Back at the apartment, my arms full of food, I want to believe again that I can convince her of my innocence. Wanting to bury the hatchet before anything could go down, I get Archie's gun, unload it, and put it back in the bag in the hallway closet. I need to give it back to Archie, it's too disturbing. I might not like weapons but I still leave the gun on the table. All the pressure accumulated these past months is slowly leaving my body and I feel like I'm deflating.

Since receiving the threatening note, I'd been living with this sword of Damocles hanging above my head. The worst thing was not knowing when the blow would come. Liliana could be thousands of miles away from New York yet I feared that she would magically materialize every corner I turn.

We are all more or less prepared to face danger, but threats are more treacherous. It creeps everywhere. We no longer look at the world the same way. Danger is permanent when it doesn't have to be. I understand why threats are an extremely effective blackmailing weapon.

I shouldn't rush until John Blatters gives me the stamp of approval, but it feels too good to believe I'm out of the woods.

I call Archie.

"Spencer, are you okay?"

93

"Yes, much better!"

"Really? Anything new?"

"Guess what!"

"You know, me and guessing…"

"The kid woke up from his coma!"

I hear a long whistle and then a short silence.

Archie clears his throat. "That's amazing! I wouldn't have bet a dollar on it."

"To be honest, neither would I. Miracles do happen…"

"Hats off to the doctors, they're getting better and better."

"Archie, don't you think this changes everything? Maybe the kid will remember what happened."

"Spencer, don't get carried away, we're still in the what-if stage. But you might be right, his mother will hear about it and it might lessen her obsession of putting a hole in you!"

"I wish. I can't stand living holed up like that. Liliana will probably hear it through the media."

"How did you find out?"

"Blatters, my shrink, he called me. He was on his way to Saint George's to see Mario. I'm waiting for him to call me back and tell me how he is."

"Let's hope for the best!"

"Fingers crossed, Archie! I'll check if the news channels are talking about it."

"Call them. You must know a journalist somewhere, don't you? It's important that they broadcast it widely, so that she hears about it quickly…"

"What if she's on the other side of the country or if she's fled abroad?"

"If she's gone, that means one less problem. Spencer, don't let your guard down. Assume that Liliana is still dangerous and behind your door until we know for sure where she is!"

"I'm sure she's run off to Cuba or Mexico or somewhere, where no one is looking for her."

Archie is insistent. "Pretend that she's behind your door and only open it when you know who's coming."

"Everyone calls me before they come up. And that's not a lot of people to begin with."

"Don't ask your friends to be brave for you. This woman is terrorizing the whole city!"

"I know that, I know that she's a real psycho. When she hears the news, she'll calm down. She has to."

"Spencer, be careful. Anything's possible with her!"

"Understood. But it was her son's coma that was driving her insane, and now that Mario is cleared, her anger is bound to drop a notch."

"You can always hope but I don't believe it too much. You're facing a goddamn psycho who won't give up!"

"Archie, she knows that staying around or trying to see her son would be fatal, she would be arrested immediately. The hospital is a fortress, and no matter how trained she is, she won't slip through the cracks for long."

"If she wants to take over the hospital, she will. One way or another. It's a hospital, not a fortress. But I'm not positive that she'll get out of there alive!"

"She knows all this, why would she want to push her luck?"

"I don't know what she's got in mind. If she does anything, it'll be one hell of a bloody mess!"

"You're forgetting that Mario's awake now. She won't do anything that could put him in danger again. She's going to forget about me for a while and go to the countryside until better times come…"

Archie doesn't answer right away, there's a long pause. I feel that he doesn't believe me.

He changes the topic and resumes in a neutral tone. "Are you able to work?"

"The editor is understanding. He gives me easy topics to work on. Writing calms me down, it keeps me from thinking too much. But now I'll be able to work more serenely again."

"Spencer, I'm your friend. If you need me, call me."

"Thanks, Archie. It's nice to know. How's Sarah?"

"Your story upset her. Especially now that she's pregnant..."

"She is? Congratulations, Archie! You guys have been talking about it for a while."

"Yeah. Time flies and it was time to stop thinking about it and to actively work on it."

"He or she is going to have great parents, as every kid should have!"

"Thanks, man. Sarah wanted to tell you herself, but with everything going on..."

"I understand. Hug her for me?"

"I will. Take care of yourself and don't forget that if there's anything suspicious, you call me!"

"Will do. Bye, Archie!"

I hang up.

The newspaper pushed me an e-mail with a topic for a paper I have to write. The topic? *Mass murders in American schools.* Liliana Morales wasn't the only murderer in this country. The usual columnist is out of office, meaning that I have to do it. The timing is perfect since a demonstration is planned for this weekend in Washington, called *March for our lives.* The new generation, born in the 2000's, is getting tired of laying flowers, saying goodbye, and burning candles after each mass killing (7,000 children killed since 2012) and are now rebelling against the NRA, the all-too powerful gun lobby.

I turn Bill, my computer, on. At first, I called it that for fun one lonely night, and it kind of stuck. Once it's powered, I lose myself deep into the virtual world, searching for trustworthy sources. Turns out there's no shortage of material on the subject and neither is the NRA's intoxication. It's the only American association that rates the senators in Congress and can destroy them with a few slanderous emails sent to their five million members. Just goes to show that the greatest democracy in the world can also be subject to mass disinformation.

I slowly sink into the killings, forgetting my own problems.

12

Today was a banal autumn morning and nothing could have foretold such an upheaval. Liliana Morales was back behind the bar of her cousin's fast-food restaurant, who was telling everyone willing to listen how badly she wanted Liliana out of the picture although she didn't mind exploiting her in the process. Having the opportunity of paying someone through accommodation and meals was rare, especially when the aforesaid person was an outstanding beautiful waitress that attracted all the thirsty males of the neighborhood like bees around a honeypot. Liliana might have been exploited, but she wasn't penniless thanks to her after-hours work. There were more and more men willing to pay for her talents, and the price went up exponentially. She was expensive enough to be able to select the wealthiest ones, making her treasure box bigger each night. She was at the bar until noon and resumed in the evening around 10 p.m. until closing time.

Today, the sky was overcast and the morning calm until Liliana opened the bar's TV and screamed at the close-up photo of her son. It was eight o'clock, rush hour, and the news channel CBS was drilling through her heart in a news flash with a picture of her son Mario waking up. The news, carefully orchestrated by the police and the media, spread like wildfire among the Cuban community. New York City was breathing again, hoping that "The Manhattan Hitwoman", every media's headline, would put an end to her killing spree.

The aforesaid person was glued to the fast-food TV and couldn't believe a word she heard. Rushing to the nearest drugstore, she bought yet another prepaid phone and called her son's hospital in a hurry, pretending to be a vague aunt. She was immediately transferred to an evasive doctor.

"Yes, the Morales kid. I'm not the one in charge, but I know he's doing much better!"

"What do you mean, he's better? Did he wake up?"

Her words were pouring from her mother's lips, almost the same ones Spencer asked John Blatters. Psychiatrists or patients, human brains and hearts react the same way to the same situation.

"As far as I know, Mario is recovering well. He's been taken off life support and machines," added the doctor.

"Did he speak?"

"He said a few words, asking for his mother."

A knife had sunk into her heart and her belly, the pain making her grunt and double over in the middle of the sidewalk where she was standing. She was speechless as the doctor continued.

"Come to the hospital! Visits are allowed now, he'll be happy to see a familiar face. It'll be good for his recovery."

It'll be a good trap to catch me too, thought Liliana, catching her breath. She felt on a barbecue grill, torn between the compelling desire to know more and the unbearable fear of being deceived.

She abruptly hung up. Something was wrong. The doctor had to be a cop, he got on the phone too quickly, never asked once who was calling and his voice was too loud. He didn't have the calm, hushed voice that hospital doctors have. It felt like he was reciting lines, that his goal was to get her to Mario's bedside. "A few words, asking for his mother"... The fucking cops were playing her, using her maternal instinct, and she almost ran straight into their trap.

Fortunately, she wasn't crazy or stupid. The feds should burn it into their brains: she wasn't a fool and knew they were waiting to pick her up at the hospital, convinced that she couldn't resist the temptation to see her son. This so-called recovery was a trick to catch her and put her back in jail.

When the TV broadcasted the news, she'd believed a miracle had happened, but quickly had to pull herself together and face the truth. This recovery was too good to be true, created in the perverted mind of a twisted cop. Mario waking up was a sham, and they'd turned her beloved son into the innocent bait of a despicable mousetrap. She promised to make those degenerate gringos pay a hundredfold for their trickery, to kill them all. To kill everyone who was keeping her little Mario and everyone who wanted her to come. She'd come – of course, she'd come. But she'd come heavily armed. Her son was still a defenseless vegetable, a guinea pig for perverted doctors who knew full well that there was no hope of recovery. She didn't want him to suffer anymore at the hands of these degenerates. She'd come loaded and prepared, not giving a damn about the people in her way. No one would be spared. She would finally be able to hold her son against her so tightly that he would be on the verge of choking, and she'd sing his favorite lullaby, cuddling him close so he wouldn't be afraid anymore. The cops wouldn't dare to do anything in case they'd hurt the child and she'd be able to leave safely with Mario in her arms, killing most – if not all – of his torturers. And, if she had to, they would both die, together, united forever.

When she returned to the restaurant, her forehead was still creased. She couldn't stand by any longer. First things first: she had to deal with the gringo responsible for all this. He wasn't the easiest to take down, and Liliana painfully finished her service with rage flaming in her stomach, deciding to kill Spencer as soon as possible. No time to eat lunch, she would be faster on an empty stomach. Hiding a long kitchen knife in her backpack, she kept the hammer used to hit Max and the old woman; it was a good weapon when you knew how to use it. It wasn't good enough against a gun, but she already knew how to get her hands on one. This was crucial since Spencer must have had at least one to defend himself. She wished she hadn't warned him. That card hadn't been thought well enough, it put her enemy out of reach. She packed her begging clothes, knowing she'd have to wait for the right moment to act. She wanted to make sure that Spencer was alone and that Archie wouldn't be in her way. Out of instinct, she was wary of this strong man with feline flexibility who walked like he was a soldier. He wouldn't be easy to surprise and fight. She put on a long sweater over a pair of jeans and sneakers, and broke into a light run, blending in with the joggers that swarmed the New York City sidewalks in the afternoon. Running would give her time to think and strengthen the plan she'd drawn up.

The facts were simple. The reporter hardly ever left his apartment anymore, and the few times he did go out, big guy Archie was always by his side. She'd learned his name and his wife's by following him home, but the doorbell only showed their first name. Since Spencer didn't want to go out, she should logically be the one to trespass into his place. It was risky, but she liked it. The first thing on her way was an armored door she'd have to take down since Spencer wouldn't let her in, no matter how beautiful she was. She was already salivating at the idea of being in front of this man who had run over her son and ran away. She'd have no pity, no compassion and she'd make him suffer enough to make him regret, to make him beg her before dying like the coward gringo that he was.

She took the subway to Manhattan without knowing that deep below New York City, exactly two hours and twenty-three minutes later, her train would cross Archie's.

That same afternoon, just as Liliana was getting off the subway, CBS News exceptionally handed the microphone to Chief Wesson Slach of the Central Police Station. His brief statement, broadcasted by most TV stations, spoke of the strong possibility that Ms. Morales had fled the United States for an unknown destination where she would no longer fear American justice.

Archie, with a beer in his hand, was sitting in front of his television, glued to the Chief's intervention like millions of New Yorkers. He jumped on his feet, cursing. He knew it wasn't true.

100

It was a feds trick to let Liliana believe that she wasn't longer America's #1 most-wanted, to let her believe she was safe and giving her enough room to make a mistake. Or, better yet, to try and go see her son. With Archie having many ties within the administration, he'd managed to call Donald, a Navy Seal working undercover for the DEA[3] the day before, who confirmed that the criminal was spotted in the city with transformed face and looks, a short-haired brunette turned a long-haired blond. Max's neighbor, a drug dealer from the Bronx, recognized her when she entered the tattoo shop and again when she left a few hours later. The feds had set up a trap that didn't work and Max was now dead, murdered a few feet from the cops.

Archie was walking in circles around his apartment while Sarah was out visiting a high school friend. He can sigh, growl and insult Liliana who was still in Manhattan all he wanted but the facts remained the same. The Navy Seal's info spun in his head all night and all morning: the threat is more real than it ever was and Archie couldn't deal with his best friend facing mortal danger.

Before making a decision, he needed all the parameters, starting with what behavior was Liliana likely to have when she learned of her son waking up. Would it change anything about her obsession? If it didn't and if revenge was what she was after, this woman would be a lifelong danger for Spencer, locked up or not. To be sure, Archie called John Blatters and asked for an urgent appointment but the secretary didn't want anything to do with him. He took a cab and arrived at the office less than fifteen minutes later, shouting loud enough for the doctor to be notified. Doc knew Archie's name thanks to Spencer and gave him ten minutes.

"I have to be honest, that woman is sick and her pathology is very disturbing –"

---

[3] The Drug Enforcement Administration (DEA) is the US federal police force under the US Department of Justice responsible for combating drug trafficking.

Archie cuts him off. He didn't come here to have a lecture on psychiatric medicine. "I only have one question for you."

"Go ahead."

"Will Liliana Morales ever let go of her revenge against Spencer?"

The doctor didn't miss a beat. "No, I don't think so."

"But her son is doing better!"

"It doesn't matter, the damage has been done and she has to punish the culprit. Spencer is not Spencer anymore, he has become a permanent threat to be eradicated. He's an obsession, a paranoid neurosis."

"Then how can we get her out of this obsession?"

"Fortunately, there are ways to improve things, but we would need to get her back to the hospital before she sinks further into her paranoia and commits other crimes."

"To be perfectly clear, you're telling me that as long as she is without treatment, her illness will get worse?"

"Yes. She knows how easy killing is, it's another means to an end. I bet she can taste blood in her mouth and enjoy it like you enjoy candy, especially since her crimes help her fool the police. It's her and her son against the world and it must be terribly pleasing to her."

He's silent for a moment before adding in a low, almost inaudible voice.

"Take care of yourself, Archie. You're often with Spencer and Liliana is aware of your friendship by now, if she's lingering around like you said."

"She is. It's been confirmed."

"Then she won't have an ounce of mercy if you get in her way. Are you married?"

"I have been for twelve years."

"That's your weakness."

"What do you mean?"

102

"Family, Archie, is the main weakness of any man or woman. Spencer is lucky to be single."

"Meaning?"

"Meaning that Liliana won't hesitate to hurt your wife to get things that she can't get on her own."

"Are you a shrink or a cop?"

"With this kind of sick person, you have to be a bit of both. But my job is to predict the reactions of the most dangerous sociopaths, which is what I've been doing for you and Spencer."

"Well, doc, you're not reassuring."

"Take your wife to a place where she'll be safe and don't forget to tell Spencer to be extremely careful. His life is at stake!"

It was at this very moment, following John Blatters' worried tone, that the only option to keep his friend safe from Liliana's vindictiveness became clear in the soldier's head. He didn't tell the psychiatrist about it, fearing he would have tried to discourage him. The news of Mario waking up wouldn't soften Liliana's need for vengeance now that she had decided to punish and kill the person responsible for the accident. There was no point in trying to prove that Spencer had nothing to do with it, she wouldn't change her mind. John Blatters had been heard loud and clear.

When Archie got back home, he'd made his mind. All that was left was preparing the next day's steps. He didn't have room for error. Sarah, who knew all about the prep having to put up with it for years when he was still in the Army, was sitting on the corner of his desk.

"What are you doing?" she asked worryingly.

"I have to take care of Spencer's safety, to protect him from that crazy woman."

"And how do you plan on protecting him with your camouflage cover and your rifle? What are you hiding from me?"

Archie began to pull apart the sniper rifle he took out of the closet, putting everything into a large bag.

He gathered his wife in his arms. "I won't be long, a quick round trip to Brooklyn to scout."

"I'm not a fool, Archie. Why do you need that rifle?"

"Wanna know the truth?"

Sarah nodded, looking serious and sad.

"I know where Liliana Morales is hiding."

"Call the cops, they'll arrest her!"

"She'll disappear before they can get close to her. The Perls gang is watching the area closely, they've got lookouts everywhere. The cops don't stand a chance."

"What's your plan then?"

"First, I'll spot the place without being spotted, it's routine. Then I'll have to make a decision, but I'm afraid I won't have much of a choice."

"What do you mean, not have much of a choice?"

"There's only one way to stop Liliana before she starts killing again."

Sarah opened her big blue eyes, understanding what her husband had decided. Her face was pasty white when she protested in a firm voice, even if she knew how useless it would be.

"Your job isn't to deal with that!"

"We're threatened too. You, me, and our baby. Spencer's psychiatrist made it clear: she won't give up. Not now, not ever."

Sarah nodded without answering. Her eyes were shining too much as she put her hands on his face, tears starting to flow between her fingers. He held her tight.

"I'm scared, Archie…"

"Trust me, honey. I have to do something before it's too late. If anything happens to you, our child, or Spencer, I could never forgive myself…"

Sarah wiped away her tears before Archie left for Brunswick. She waited for him to come home to fall asleep, her body pressed against his. He didn't want to talk about his trip. That night, they made love like they used to just before he got deployed, and it left a bitter taste in their mouths and hearts.

13

The evening came too soon for Sarah. She watched her husband prepare his equipment and put everything in the bag before leaving a loaded gun in the living room coffee table's drawer. Right by it, he left his ID, his tag, his keys, and the picture of Sarah he always kept on him.

"I won't be long but we'd better be safe than sorry, right?"

"I don't like any of it, Archie!"

"Do you remember how to use it?"

"Yes, but I don't like guns…"

"The job will be done by tonight. In the meantime, go to your sister's house, you'll be safe there. I'll call you when I get back."

He kissed Sarah and she insisted on walking him to the subway station, grabbing his arm. As they passed the building where Liliana was holed up, Archie took a quick look at the spot where the old woman who had been squatting there for months was begging. He thought that there was something different about her, that she didn't look quite the same as usual. Sarah slipped her arm under his. He pulled her close one last time and, as she watched him walk down the stairs to the station, a gut-wrenching feeling settled in her stomach.

It's rush hour, and the Manhattan workers are going home. In the crowded subway, no one notices the man wearing a long-hooded coat that sits at the back of the train, quietly reading a tabloid. Far from downtown Manhattan's towers, Brooklyn is getting ready for a cold night. The north wind blows in light gusts. Barely out of the subway, Archie keeps close the walls all the way to 222 Brunswick Avenue. There are too many people on the streets at this time of the day. Not thinking twice about using the elevator, he silently goes up the stairs to the door leading to the terrace, struggling to unlock it with the master key. Before stepping on the terrace, he checks his outfit one last time, puts on his gloves so he wouldn't leave any fingerprints, lowers his beanie on his forehead so he wouldn't leave a single hair on the scene, and crawls to his ambush spot between two air vents. He barely has enough room to lie down. Everything is true to what he'd seen on the military topography site that had a precision of more or less 9.8 inches. When the night falls, he's just where he had planned.

From his vantage point, Archie has a view of the Brunswick crossroads. Across the street, the glass door to the Diaz's fast-food is brightly lit. The overcast, moonless weather is perfect for what Archie wants to do. He opens the bag containing the rifle, the main tool of the sniper soldier he'd been in Afghanistan and Iraq. The stock of the rifle is worn and the varnish frosted where he presses his cheek to stabilize and aim. It's a 50 caliber – a philistine couldn't even start to imagine the damages that this weapon makes. The recoil would knock down an untrained man. Tonight, the McMillan Tac-50, also known as Mk15, is loaded with A-Max low-drag bullets, fireflies propelled at several times the speed of sound. The air glides over them with no drag or deflection.

It's been a long time since Archie fired a shot and adrenaline stalls at his fingertips. Mechanically, breathing deeply, he raises the gun without hesitation, the movement anchored deep in his memory. He adjusts the monocular with precision and, despite the light wind, he raises it to neutral. The restaurant jumped towards him from 1,171 feet away. Even a beginner wouldn't miss this target. He can clearly see the customers, the tables, the chairs, the bar, and the bottles at the back.

Liliana arrives at 10 p.m. at the earliest to take her cousin's place, who always heads home shortly after. The soldier chooses

108

to fire at this exact moment. He'll only have a few seconds to hit the bull's eye since patrons always crowd the front of the bar as soon as she stands behind it. He can't risk hurting a customer. His hand cannot shake.

He's been deployed so much that he's not even surprised to find himself there, waiting under his camouflage blanket on top of a New York City building to kill someone. He didn't tell Spencer about the mission; he would have refused Liliana's cold-blooded execution. But in Archie's military-trained mind, attacking before being attacked is self-defense. He's carried out many other operations, often more dangerous and more traumatic. This one will not feed his post-traumatic syndrome one bit. For once, he's sure that his conscience wouldn't bug him. His family is being threatened: he's doing whatever it takes to protect them, just like he did for his brothers during the war. That's the way the world works, the strong annihilates the weak, one way or another. His past life as a sniper had taught him that hesitating increased the danger, meaning that he swallowed a bunch of beta-blockers pills to slow down his heart before leaving. Two more hours to wait before he could end this.

Light rain falls on the city and the cold sweeps in, making Archie pull the camouflage cover over his head. In the grey concrete, the long black gun is a color break. Birds brush past it without noticing. The sniper soldier is on the lookout, his eye riveted to the scope of his rifle.

Waiting patiently.

But tonight, Liliana Morales isn't in Brunswick and is likely to be late for her shift. She's been dressing like an old lady for almost a month, begging in the late afternoon close to Spencer's building. The place is ideal to watch who gets in and out of the building and keep tabs on Archie. She'll skin the man alive and his inability to let her roam around, and, if she had to, she'll also kill his pretty wife Sarah who rarely leaves their apartment right behind Spencer's building. She keeps on watching the door, waiting for the right moment. This woman is eager for the smell of blood, like a wild beast on the lookout. Nothing will distract her.

The long-awaited moment finally arrives. She sees Archie and Sarah come out of the dead-end by the building. The tall man is carrying a long bag over his shoulder, looking like he's going on a trip. Which means that Spencer is alone in his ivory tower. Only a fool would let the opportunity to act fly by without acting on it. Liliana waits for the couple to disappear around the corner and she gathers the few things she owns in her backpack before disappearing in the dead-end. Archie and Sarah's door is easy to pick.

It doesn't take her long to find what she was looking for. She didn't come here by chance, positive that this martial-looking guy must have some weapons hidden somewhere. Upon discovering the secured cabinet, she knows that she was right. Of course, it's locked and without the code, there's no way she can open it. She's raging, insulting Archie and his wife before remembering that every good American hides at least one gun within reach, most of the time in their room. Liliana turns over the bed, empties the closets and the wardrobe. When she comes back in the living room dejected and swearing, she knocks over the coffee table. The drawer opens, revealing a picture, keys, and an ID while the gun slides on the carpet.

With a cry of joy, she throws herself on the weapon, checks its magazine, and, with the Colt in her hand, she walks to the kitchen and drinks straight from the tap. The first part of the plan is a success. She has a gun – all there's left to do is wait for Sarah's husband to return.

With a smile, Liliana slumps into Archie's armchair that sits in front of the door. She crosses her long legs hard enough to feel pain and waits, a pillow tight against her belly to hide her hand tightened on the gun. She doesn't mind waiting, loving the exaltation that builds up before she kills. It's an explosive pleasure to hold someone's life, someone's destiny between your hands. To be able to end their life in the blink of an eye, to hold such divine power. Taking someone's life has something infinitely more orgasmic than giving it. Nothing could beat this feeling.

When Sarah enters, she freezes on the threshold at the sight of Liliana Morales sitting in her husband's chair. She would have recognized the face with the unblinking eyes that were on every news channel anywhere. She opens her mouth but she doesn't scream: a bullet coming out of the gun at the speed of sound slices through her head before she can even realize it. The sound of the detonation is lost in the pillow that Liliana holds close, the synthetic feathers flying up to the ceiling.

The killer watches Sarah collapse, letting out another cry of joy with her finger still clenched around the trigger, drool forming at the corners of her strangely extinct smile. Sarah moans and Liliana is almost happy about it; her death would have been too quick otherwise. The more Liliana kills, the more she likes it. Sarah has a sudden body spasm that uncovers her upper legs, a flood of blood oozing from her skull. The extraordinary indecency of Sarah's death hits Liliana, who jumps from her seat and throws what remains of the pillow on the head of her victim to hide it.

Sarah came back alone – she must have walked her husband to the subway before returning. Archie was probably long gone by now. That's too bad, she would have liked to see him fall over his wife from the blow of the still-warm gun in her hand and watch the dead couple pile into an obscene mount. Her enemies' friends were her enemies. Archie will get what's coming for him soon enough but, in the meantime, there's still a lot to do before going back to Brooklyn. Getting rid of her clothes and her poor underwear, she steps over the body in all her naked glory and heads towards Sarah's closet. She wants a new skin again. Liliana puts on black stockings, a set of dark red underwear, an off-white lace blouse, and a grey suit skirt that's a

111

bit narrow on her waist but should work, given that she's about Sarah's size. Small-heeled pumps on her feet, she brushes her hair and does her makeup in front of the mirror. When she's ready, Liliana puts the warm Colt in her handbag and a satisfied smile on her lips, straightens her spine, and holds her head high. She's almost there, her revenge is close. As soon as she's outside, she speeds to Spencer's building in a rapidly falling night.

Stripped of her rags, Liliana Morales is an elegant woman that most men would love to have waiting for them at home every night. Pretending that her parking pass didn't work, she charmed the underground parking lot's guard and got through the gate to the elevators serving the entire building.

When the elevator door opens on an odd floor, showing a couple that doesn't look twice at her, she patiently waits for them to exit before entering slowly, just like she's entering a sacred place that sends shivers run through her spine. With her short-nailed fingers, she presses button 17, Spencer's floor.

When she steps out of the elevator, the dimensions of the vast paneled marble landing surprise her. Obviously, the door to Spencer's apartment is locked and unpickable. Ringing the doorbell wouldn't do her any favor: she knew that Archie wasn't there but it didn't mean that Spencer was alone and it would be the easiest way to warn him. The camera in the doorbell must cover the entire landing and hiding would only alert him. Because Liliana was prepared for this eventuality, she went up the stairs to the upper floor. She had to choose between the three landing doors, but it was the one leading to the apartment above Spencer's that interested her. She rings the doorbell and a middle-aged housekeeper in working clothes greets her. With a smile, Liliana pretends to stumble, clings to her apron, and pushes her brutally inside, covering her mouth with one hand before breaking her neck with the other. The two women, dead and living, fall tightly entwined.

Before getting up, Liliana stays still, attentive, but not a single noise comes from the apartment. Relieved of her silent effectiveness, she shuts the door with her foot and keeps lying by her victim's body heat for a long moment. This warm mass under her makes her think of her mom, Dora, when she used to put Liliana on her belly in the mornings. It had been a while since she'd thought about her mother. She dwells on the feeling and remains motionless, snuggled by this woman who doesn't breathe anymore; there's still no noise in the apartment giving someone's presence away. When Liliana finally gets up, she's come to her senses and shamelessly looks at the slumped body of the old employee. Time flies: it's almost nighttime and she needs to get the plan moving. Stepping out on the eighteenth-floor terrace, she looks at the distant avenue below and the tiny yellow cabs that follow one another with their headlights lit. It's a good thing she's not afraid of heights because she'll have to climb over the railing, hang herself and give her body enough momentum to jump onto Spencer's recessed terrace without missing the landing. *Difficult but possible*, she coldly assesses. A light rain starts falling again and she can't wait any longer or the concrete will be too slippery. Liliana leans over one last time to evaluate the risks even though she's used to this kind of exercise, and grimaces before putting her suit jacket and her shoes in her bag. Ready and determined, skirt pulled up over her hips, uncovering her black stockings, she looks up at the sky, crosses her chest, and steps over the railing.

On the lower floor, Spencer is sitting at his kitchen table, sipping coffee. His mood is broody and he's cold, shivering from a light breeze. *I should go and close the French windows, the night will be cold*, he thinks as he praises the rain that will water the oleanders on his terrace that he always forgets.

Liliana's knuckles hurt from hanging on the ledge, supporting all her weight. Hanging in the air, she begins to swing, aiming for Spencer's terrace, but feels her fingers slipping a little

113

more with each movement. At some point, her fingers would let go and she'll have to brace for the impact.

Spencer is concerned: after the euphoria that followed Mario's news, his joy has faded. This woman doesn't work like everyone else and Archie had called him back to go over the whole *"Don't open to anyone but me"* once again. The tension is back. Hoping to forget about the situation for a little bit, he raids his fridge, a glass of good scotch in his hand that will undoubtedly cheer him up. He's over being a target waiting to be shot and decides to leave the next day for a chalet in the mountains where no one will look for him. This decision makes him feel better.

Liliana's landing on the wet tiles was difficult, as expected, but as soon as she hits the terrace she's already trespassing in Spencer's living room with her fingers wrapped around the gun and her naked feet wetting the hardwood floor. She comes further in, her head held high and her stare unblinking, livid under the make-up, jaw tight. She's finally made it. She can feel that Spencer is here, the smell invading her nostrils. *The pig is drinking his last coffee,* she tells herself, and saliva pools in her mouth. She hears the familiar sound of a fridge opening, the tinkling of glass, and the sound of liquid being poured. She thinks of her son that would soon be avenged. The murderer is here, right next to her, and she slowly walks towards the kitchen, singing the lullaby she sang to put her son to sleep with a hoarse voice. She wants him to hear her coming, to understand that his death is looming. Her hatred is too strong to kill him without him knowing it. The words jostle between her lips as she sings louder but the noises have stopped. Nothing but silence can be heard. *Now,* she seethes, *he knows...* When she appears in the kitchen doorway before she can even see Spencer, her finger brushes across the trigger of her gun, securing the grip that makes her moan with pleasure.

14

10:30 p.m. in Brooklyn.

Posted on the roof of the building and under the camouflage cover, Archie hasn't moved since the night fell. The pigeons, disturbed at first, have since landed around him and almost forgotten he existed. The neighborhood is quiet and the watchmen, the dealers weren't there yet. Liliana was late but she shouldn't be long. Downstairs, behind her bar, Pepita is raging and getting impatient, often looking at her watch.

"What is this slut doing? She should have been there half an hour ago!"

The restaurant is full, and several customers have already asked where Liliana was. Her success wasn't pleasing Pepita, who replied curtly – she envied her cousin. Upstairs, on the building's terrace, Archie is as calm as one can get in this kind of situation, coming slowly to his senses. During his previous missions, he spent hours hiding under that same cover, waiting patiently for the target to appear before his trained eyes. The smell, a mixture of gun oil and human sweat, is familiar. He didn't have any other choice but to wait. Patience was the ultimate weapon, the one you could only get with time. Being one with your surroundings, being as unmoving as stone, being as dry as the desert, as vegetal as the forest, as concrete as the ground of this terrace: he knew to do all that. Camouflage, pushed to its paroxysm, is the art of concealment that requires, beyond composure and nerves of steel, months of training and years of experience. The recipe is simple: melt like sugar in water and forbid yourself to move or to blink because the slightest movement in a motionless environment can be spotted from miles away. Archie, under his blanket, remembers everything.

He doesn't know why, probably a predatory instinct, but despite the insane risks and the tough fights, even if he's not that proud of it, he loves being a state-approved killer.

The steel of the rifle is cold. With his thumb, he regularly cleans the scope that the evening rain fogs. All is quiet; the birds don't pay attention to this formless, motionless shape, lying between two big conical vents.

An hour had passed and Archie thought that she wouldn't come. Worry twisted his guts until he saw Liliana exit a cab in a hurry and rush into the restaurant. He wasn't sure it was her at first, her blondness surprising him. Fortunately, a Navy-Seal working for the DEA called Donald had warned him: she was barely recognizable. She wasn't dressed as expected – too chic, not her style. Feminine outfits weren't Archie's style but the suit's cut was somewhat familiar to him. The Cuban was definitely becoming Americanized. As soon as she entered the room, the pretty waitress was greeted by laughter and dubious jokes from patrons pressing at the bar. Pepita grabbed her arm and scolded her for being late but the killer easily escaped her grasp and didn't listen to the lecture. Nobody knew how she was still savoring her vengeful trip, how she was indulging in the intense pleasure of having massacred – well, not quite but almost – the person responsible for her son's downfall. She left Spencer dying on the kitchen floor, two bullets in the stomach. The first lodged in his gut, the second in his liver. A double shot ensures a certain but very slow death. With wounds like these, he would suffer for hours before bleeding out. The agony would be slow and excruciating. As a precaution, she tied him to the radiator and gagged him so he couldn't call for help. The goal was to have him spend the night agonizing before dying at dawn. Liliana would think about him all night, about what he was feeling, wishing she could feel his pain to be sure that it was truly unbearable. She'd like to taste her revenge, to savor the death of this degenerate that would always be too soft. When she took off Sarah's suit jacket, it was no longer an item of clothing but a trophy that she hung on the coat rack. Dismissing the lewd remarks thrown her way by a few customers on the heavier side, she slipped behind the bar and took her shift with a usual smile on her lips.

Up there, under his camouflage blanket, Archie shivers but it's not from cold, more from a bad feeling in his gut. He crosses his chest as well and, with his thumb, unlocks the safety on his gun. The young woman's face is now framed in the high-resolution scope. The wind is low and the rifle is set at 300. Archie holds his breath and lets his index finger slide over the trigger. He knows this tiny shift well. It's the last thing on the to-do list, the one that changes everything.

Despite the silencer, pigeons fly away just after the first bullet shatters the front door glass and catapults Liliana against the mirrors behind the bar. Hit in the chest, her mouth is wide open, gulping for air. She tries to stand up but the second bullet, which was shot before the first one even hit her, blazes through her forehead and comes back emptying her skull.

Deadly shot, Liliana slides down slowly, leaving a bloody trail against the mirror before collapsing behind the bar. Archie stays unmoving for a moment, eyes riveted to the monocular, just to be sure. But he knows from experience that nobody could survive these wounds. Pigeons land on the roof terrace next door. Still lying down, Archie picks up the two scorching-hot shells and puts them in his pocket. He quickly pulls his rifle apart and crawls to the door so that no one can see him. He knows that not a single soul will be able to guess where the hitman was posted since the shot's echo got bumped from one building to another. But he knows how to better be safe than sorry, and doesn't want to be greeted by the Perls' lookouts when he exits the building. Archie is walking down the street when he hears the first police sirens. The cops pass him and stop their SUV at the Brunswick intersection, in front of the restaurant where the last customers are escaping.

Hurrying, Archie turns around the corner and speeds up; he needs to avoid police controls. It would be complicated to explain why he has a rifle in his over-the-shoulder bag and why he smells like gunpowder – a smell that any cop would immediately identify. He needs to get rid of the evidence quickly, throw the shells in one of the East River swamps, and burn his clothes, bag, blanket, jacket, and shoes that must be dusted with the terrace's concrete. You'd be amazed at what the police labs can detect. The bullets in the wall behind the bar should soon start talking and the Mk15 wasn't a common weapon. Forensics will quickly identify the source, model, year, and type of ammunition, which will initially narrow their search to serving military and New York City veterans. However, it'll be a moment before they find him, giving Archie enough time to get rid of any trace of gunpowder and clothing items he wore tonight, erasing all evidence from his nightly expedition. Sarah will swear that he'd stayed in the apartment all night. The hardest will be to part from his rifle, from his faithful buddy that saved his life more often than not. This might be the ultimate gift he'll give to Spencer. It's not coming as a surprise, he knew that he'd have to sacrifice his gun since the split second he decided to neutralize Liliana.

"*Neutralize – another military term to avoid saying killing,*" Spencer would have said.

As of right now, the McMillan beats against his hip in a re-assuring rhythm, and Archie fears he won't have the courage to throw it in the swamp. It's more than a gun, it's a war buddy, the most faithful among the most faithful, the ultimate protector. Fifteen minutes later, Archie rushes into the nearest subway station with his cap pulled down low over his forehead, a newspaper in hand to fool surveillance cameras. Mingling lightheart-edly with the crowd waiting on the platform, he's unaware of the tragedies that happened in the City.

When the train starts, Archie is standing up, wedged against the back of a seat, thinking that he'd just turned a kid into an orphan, that life will be hard for Mario, but maybe not as hard as it could have been if his mother was still alive. You can never know which way the scale will tip; his past military life proved it many times.

He's now thinking about Sarah and the baby nestled in her belly, thinking how eager he is to see her and see Spencer again. Realizing that he saved him from death makes Archie smile widely, that same smile that firemen have coming back from a big fire they'd finally put out. However, a small insignificant de-tail suddenly catches his eye. Huge advertising posters dedicated to women's fashion are plastered on the walls of the station.

Something blows up in Archie's brain. The image of Liliana behind the bar just before he fired comes forcefully back to him like a boomerang. He sees again the embroidery that he took as a reference to adjust his first shot.

The same embroidery that is displayed on the panels, and the same one that Sarah has on one of her blouses. Feeling his heart speed and the train accelerate, Archie sits down brutally, the weight of the doubt too heavy for his body, his eyes wide open as he watches the gloomy, endless procession of neon lights in the tunnel.

CPSIA information can be obtained
at www.ICGtesting.com
Printed in the USA
LVHW030703170522
718962LV00001B/115